THE GUNS OF PERALTA

THE GUNS OF PERALTA

Richard Clarke

Walker and Company
New York

First published in the United States of America in 1994
by Walker Publishing Company, Inc.

Published simultaneously in Canada by Thomas Allen & Son
Canada, Limited, Markham, Ontario

Library of Congress Cataloging-in-Publication Data
Clarke, Richard, 1916–
The guns of Peralta/Richard Clarke.
p. cm.
ISBN 0-8027-1275-4
I. Title.
PS3566.A34G86   1994
813'.54—dc20   93-22963
CIP

Printed in the United States of America

2 4 6 8 10 9 7 5 3 1

CHAPTER ONE
Early Spring

FOR SLIGHTLY OVER two months, all the border communities existed in a period of apprehension. Revolutions in Mexico were common. Communities farther north of the border had less to worry about. The towns such as Peralta, whose Mex-town inhabitants had ties with Old Mexico and where the distance to the border with Mexico was no more than a short day's ride, knew from experience how easily those wars in Mexico could cross territorial boundaries. Often, when one side or the other was defeated, the victors pursued the vanquished in all directions, including across the line into U.S. territory where, by mutual agreement, the organized armed forces of both nations were forbidden to trespass. The arrangement was not always respected by Mexican forces, and was never respected by ragtag revolutionaries, whose insurrections frequently collapsed. Defeated revolutionaries fled to the sanctuary of U.S. soil because Mexican law stated that anyone rising against the federal government who was "taken bearing arms" was to be executed within fifteen minutes of apprehension.

In Peralta as in all other border communities, news of uprisings down over the line caused much anxiety. Merchants suffered, freight and stage lines curtailed normal activities, and people lived from day to day in a state of justifiable fear.

But the spring of 1892 arrived without any turmoil nearby. Rains came to the south desert. Grass grew, wild-flowers flourished, the days were glass-clear and warm, the nights were star-bright, and people slept without fear.

Mexican-town, which was the original Peralta, located behind Gringo-town on the east side, was the most reliable source of information about conditions below the line. When there were not any rumors, people sat under frond *ramadas* on warm evenings, children played, the cantina had music, and the inhabitants of Gringo-town could be at peace, or, as those who spoke Spanish said, people could "rest tranquil."

For the border communities it was a time for thanksgiving, although few actually gave thanks. Merchants, for example, simply exploited the period of peace by expanding their trade, lawmen chased the individual bandit, and cattlemen who came south for the few months of strong graze and browse arrived with their armed riders, prepared for trouble that seemed not to exist.

Because New Mexico Territory was not a state, and territories were administered by the military, town lawmen were either local constables or town marshals, and their authority ordinarily did not extend beyond the limits of their town, although they generally filled the void in outlying areas where there was no military, which was to say perhaps as much as one-half or two-thirds of New Mexico. It was an arrangement neither the citizens nor the army had difficulty accepting.

The town marshal in Peralta was a tall, lean, stringy Texan named Lee Custis. He had been marshal less than six months, but already had a reputation as a rawhide-tough man whose most noteworthy ability thus far had been the way he maintained order with his fists more often than with his gun.

Those cattlemen who came south every spring learned early that shooting up Peralta, or being troublesome for other reasons, got those who were too drunk to stand locked up; those whose imbibing had instilled in them a conviction that they were ten feet tall and bullet-proof ended up with some fractured ribs, a broken nose, or a swollen jaw.

Lee Custis was a likable, slow-talking, good-natured individual. He had pale-blue eyes, a shock of sun-bleached light-brown hair, and although he stood about six feet in his boots, he was not noticeably muscular or, as far as that went, particularly intimidating in appearance. But he had rock-hard, lightning-fast fists, and upon the one occasion when he'd had to use his belt gun, he had been fast and deadly accurate.

The most notable thing about him among the people of Peralta was that while he was a good listener, he never talked about himself. That did not stop the rumors from blossoming, including a story that he had been a Texas ranger, that he had abandoned a wife in Texas, and that he was a reformed horse thief. (Lee was never a ranger. He was a widower and he had run down his share of horse thieves without ever being tempted to follow that unhealthy vocation himself.)

Lee Custis fit in, whether it was at Mike Kelly's Gringo-town saloon or the cantina of Juan Morales in Mex-town. He had learned some Spanish growing up in Texas. Having been a rangeman, he could talk cattle and horses with the stockmen.

He was, as Mike Kelly had said, the most promising lawman Peralta'd had since Mike could remember, and that went back quite a few years.

Armand Sommers, for some reason known as "Foggy," the liveryman and horse trader, was particularly respectful of the town marshal. Someone had stolen three horses from his corral behind the barn one night, and although Lee was gone three days, he brought all three horses back, along with a fourth horse carrying a disreputable-looking, unshaven, unwashed dead man. He simply said he found the horse thief camped in an arroyo where his supper fire wouldn't show, gave him a chance to surrender, and when the horse thief had chosen instead to fight, Lee had shot him through the head.

Thus far in his tenure as Peralta's town marshal, the dead horse thief was his only kill, but it made quite an impression.

Early spring was a wonderful time to be alive on the south desert. There was none of the debilitating heat that would come later, the land was green and fragrant with small flowers, livestock got tallow under their hides, merchants flourished. *Arrieros* from Mexico came in pack trains drawn by tough Mexican mules. Big freight wagons, with especially wide tires to prevent too much settling into the earth under heavy loads, ground their way through, mostly from up north where the territory's commerce originated. And outside of town, stockmen whose camps were usually close to some source of water were settled in for the grazing season.

Above all this was a flawless turquoise sky. Later it would be a malevolent pale shade around a pitiless sun.

Peralta was prepared for a pleasant spring and a tolerable summer. In Mex-town, buildings were of mud with walls three feet thick, keeping the temperature inside those adobe buildings at least fifteen degrees cooler than outside.

On both sides of the main thoroughfare in Gringo-town, the majority of buildings had been made of wood. People who worked or lived in such structures suffered from the heat, the occasional wild desert winds, and feared fire above almost everything else. Their buildings became tinder-dry during the hot time of the year, and while Peralta's long-forgotten founders had created their original village around two excellent wells, what few fires that had occurred had resulted in complete destruction because town water brigades, using buckets handed from man to man, were incapable of putting out a dry-wood fire.

One of those wells was in the center of Mex-town's dusty plaza. It had a wall of adobe bricks waist high to prevent animals and children from falling in. It also had two logs set into the ground on each side, with a strong cross-member adjoining them from which was suspended an ancient wooden block that turned when the bucket was lowered and pulled to the top, full of water.

The well in Gringo-town had the same arrangement for drawing water, but with a reinforced steel cross-member and a steel pulley for drawing water. It was located on the west side of town in a small area kept clear of obstructions, and while women drew water for washing and cleaning, they rarely lingered, as opposed to the well in Mex-town, where the women did their laundry, gossiped, minded children, and made something of a ritual of congregating there.

The gathering place for men in Mex-town was Juan Morales's cantina. Juan was a dark, thickset man graying at the temples. His cantina had one deeply recessed window in the wall facing the plaza. There was no glass. Once, years earlier, there had been a paper-thin scraped patch of rawhide that allowed light in but through which it was impossible to see. Juan had torn it out, put wooden shutters outside in case of rain or high winds, but ordinarily from spring to late summer the shutters were locked open. With one door and only one window, the building was somewhat of a fort.

The cantina had a number of rough tables and chairs. Unlike the saloon in Gringo-town, men sat, smoked, talked, and sipped everything from aguardiente to mescal. It was more a place to meet than to seriously drink.

Six years before Lee Custis arrived, there had been a wild brawl started by six *arrieros* out of Mexico, complete with tiny copper bells on their trousers. They were dark, sweaty young men who drank too much and called the Peralta Mexicans such names as dogs of the *gringos,* lazy donkeys, even riders of other people's horses.

When the screaming and destruction ended, Juan had three dead *arrieros* to drag outside, two demolished tables to replace, and six shattered chairs.

Since that time, Juan kept a sturdy ash wagon spoke beneath his bar, a sawed-off shotgun beside the spoke, and was disinclined to show hospitality to strangers from south of the border.

He and Gringo-town's saloonman, Mike Kelly, were close friends. Kelly and Juan Morales would occasionally, with no prior announcement to their patrons, lock up and go hunting together. Neither of them was married, neither was entirely dedicated to regular hours or community service. Despite the difference in skin shade, they were more alike in the ways that mattered than most men in the Peralta countryside.

Lee Custis joined them occasionally, hunting or playing pedro or poker. Some people did not quite approve of friendships between whites and Mexicans, but generally people in both parts of town ignored the relationship. Lee, Mike, and Juan did not care what people thought.

It was a good spring, peaceful and abundant in rain for maize, grass for livestock, and no sign of trouble below the border.

Marshal Custis leaned on Mike Kelly's bar one afternoon, content and satisfied. Mike, who came closest of the pair to being a cynic, finally sounded a jarring note when he said, "Well, I been down here close to fifteen years." His eyes narrowed a little. "When it's this peaceful an' all, someone or some*thing*—Gawd or the devil, or maybe just fate—can't abide it."

The town marshal laughed.

Kelly fixed him with a sulfurous look. "Wait an' see. I'm older'n you; whatever steers us through this life just plain can't stand havin' things go along peaceful very long."

CHAPTER TWO
A Hint of Change

IT WAS THE custom in the borderlands, where villages and towns were far apart with no way to communicate except by horseback, to establish large mounds of dry greasewood some distance from each community.

The alternative was to have sentinels out yonder who might desert their posts because of boredom.

The purpose of those heaps of faggots was to spread the alarm if attackers appeared. The dark, oily smoke from greasewood fires could be seen for miles. The original idea had been to give warning when bands of Indian warriors—Apaches, Comanches, Tarahumares, and Yaquis up out of Mexico—roamed the Southwest killing, torturing, stealing, and burning.

By 1892, Mexico's Indians found it less troublesome to raid at home, particularly during revolutions. Comanches and Apaches had fought themselves almost to the point of extinction. They were still active, but not as they had been when Mike Kelly and other old-timers in Peralta had slept with one eye open.

Now the faggot mounds were kept replenished for a different kind of marauder: bands of renegades, whose numbers were frequently as high as twenty or thirty men. They were a merciless, savage lot: white bandits, Mexican *bandoleros*, half-breed Indians, homeless Confederates, men with bounties on their heads. Deadly, fierce, murderous,

7

totally amoral individuals who believed in nothing but bloodletting and burning, stealing and torturing. They became the scourge of the frontier, riding at a run, often half drunk, armed to the teeth, unshaven, unwashed, screaming like madmen when they rode into a village with the sun at their backs.

Every army post, camp, or station between east Texas and far western New Mexico Territory worked soldiers to skin and bones in a largely unsuccessful attempt to annihilate outlaw armies.

Supreme authority throughout the Territory was the army. It did its utmost, which was never adequate as marauder bands increased, burned, murdered, tortured almost with impunity. Pleas to Washington for more Gatling guns, horse soldiers and horses, more and better rifles, produced negligible results. The result was predictable: the disaffected on both sides of the border and from within Indian reservations—outlaws, misfits, fugitives—formed more marauding bands, until the entire Southwest lived in holy dread.

Shortly before a perfect springtime yielded to stifling summer, marauders in considerable numbers struck a village called Aromanches sixty miles northwest of Peralta.

A lone survivor, a child whose parents had hidden him in a hole, told the grisly tale to a patrol of horse soldiers.

There were adobe buildings standing, because mud did not burn. Everything else had been destroyed. Thirty-six corpses were found of an actual count of sixty people said to have lived in Aromanches. The others were never found.

The devastation was complete. Aside from the little boy, there was not a living thing left when the soldier patrol rode in. Not even dogs or chickens.

The child's story horrified everyone who heard it. After entering Aromanches, the raiders collected weapons, piled them inside a wooden structure, then lined up the inhabitants. Those who hesitated to tell where they had hidden money or jewelry were tortured until they screamed for mercy and told where their caches were. Then everyone was shot at close range by marauders who had spent an hour depleting the supply of liquor in the village's only cantina.

As word of the atrocity spread, a number of people abandoned the south desert entirely and moved miles away. Those who remained lived in dread.

When they heard, Mike Kelly squinted at Lee Custis across his bar and said, "I told you. The springtime was too perfect to last. It's goin' to be a bad summer."

Lee went down to Mex-town. Juan Morales shrugged thick shoulders when Lee asked if he'd heard who the marauders were. "No one knows. They didn't come over the line." Juan ran a sour damp rag across the counter and scowled. There were several older men at tables, as silent as stones, looking and listening to every word mentioned at the bar.

Juan had a question of his own. "Afterwards, which way did they go?"

The constable had no idea. So far he had met no one who would know.

Juan gave his bartop another vigorous sweep. "Do you know how far Aromanches was from Peralta? No more than sixty miles." He leaned for emphasis. "If they scouted up Aromanches, more than likely they know where Peralta is."

Lee had already thought about this. The marshal said, "I've got a feller atop the general store with a spyglass. I found a couple of fellers to mind the signal mounds." Lee sighed. "So much for peace and good weather. At least it's not a horde of routed *bandoleros* from down yonder."

"Worse," stated Juan Morales. Behind him the silent listeners nodded their heads. One of them removed a pipe and spoke in Spanish.

"Night guards. They often come in the dark."

Lee had no experience with marauders, but over the years he had heard a number of stories, and they were all the same. If possible, not a living thing was left after an attack. Women were carried away, never to be heard of again. Branded horses turned up as far away as California and Mexico City.

One of the older men removed his pipe to comment in Spanish. "Hark you, they are clever, many times more clever than we are. Take it to heart, companions, it is said they charge out of the sun, but let me tell you, riders who know enough to have the sun in the faces of those they attack are not simply drunken killers. You understand?"

No one replied. One by one the old men rose and departed. As Lee watched them go, he told himself that by suppertime everyone in Peralta would be frightened out of their wits.

Juan also watched the old men leave. He said, "There are other towns. They could raid in any direction."

Lee gazed at his friend. "That should make us feel better?"

A very attractive Mexican woman appeared in the cantina doorway, which was as far as she was allowed. Custom and tradition decreed that women could not enter the cantina. She spoke in swift Spanish to Juan Morales and ignored Lee Custis. She was gone before Morales addressed the town marshal. "You see? Already everyone knows. The two men she named are going to scout northward."

Lee had understood every word the woman had said. His only comment was dry and tart. "Two scouts, moving in open country where nothing else is moving, could damn well never come back."

He left the cantina, went back to Gringo-town, where he encountered the large, graying, and expressionless man who owned the general store, the largest and most profitable enterprise in Peralta. His name was George Franklin, but he was called by the rank he had held in the Union army, "Cap." Every Independence Day when men paraded, Cap wore his bronze-star medal.

Lee did not expect anxiety from Cap, and he got none. The large older man said, "I tried to buy a Gatling gun last summer. It had to have been stolen from the army, but I thought someday it might be handy."

"What happened?"

"The man I agreed to give a hundred dollars for it was hauling it to Peralta when an army patrol stopped him without a word. They pulled the canvas top off his rig and there it was. They had him turn around and go away with them."

Lee's gaze wandered. Men who during the normal course of their business days never went armed, were girdled with shellbelts and holstered pistols.

Cap said, "If nothing happens for a few days, things will get back to normal." He, too, watched the armed citizens of Peralta. His next words were as dry as old wood. "Excitement don't last."

Later, Lee went to the lower end of town where the livery barn and corrals were located. Foggy Sommers had shoved back the hat he wore, which had a two-inch brim slightly curled, and was scratching his stomach. He looked up, stopped scratching, and smiled. "How are they takin' it in Mex-town?"

"About like folks are up here."

Foggy was a short, rotund man, shrewd and not the kind of an individual who would readily succumb to rumors or excitement. In a country where hat brims were wide enough to protect the face and back of the head from fierce summer heat, his little curly-brimmed derby looked ridiculous.

"Seems to me," he said, "folks is like chickens. They get upset and act silly. If them marauders raided Aromanches, which is fifty, sixty miles from Peralta, why then they got ten different directions to go, and that'd make their chances of comin' down here ten to one. Pretty big odds, wouldn't you say?"

"Big odds," Lee replied. "Unless Peralta is *the* one out of ten. . . . You got a bug bite?"

"Something. Danged belly button's been itching like hell last few days." He reset his derby and wagged his head. "I been through a hunnert of these scares, an' out of that number only once did trouble even come close. . . . That was in Missouri when a band of Kansas jayhawkers snuck up on our village in the night." Foggy paused to look up and slyly smile. "We had wolf traps sprung open at both ends of town. When them things commenced goin' off everyone run out with rifles. . . . They never come back." Foggy's expression brightened. "Marshal, that's what we ought to do."

Lee nodded. "Good idea. Where do we get wolf traps?"

Foggy's inspired expression soured. He even stopped scratching.

Lee went up to the café, where all the gossip of other times had been banished in favor of what the men seemed convinced was going to happen within the next few days.

Lee could tell them nothing beyond what they already knew: Peralta was an armed camp with spies on the rooftops and men out yonder ready to fire the signal mounds at first sight of massed riders.

One man, a vinegary individual who owned the harness works, made a pithy comment about the people over in Mex-town, his implication being that they would secretly meet the marauders and maybe even lead them into town.

No one commented about that, but several diners, including the town marshal and the saloonman, gave the harness maker a hard look.

It was the approach of dusk that seemed to bring with it degrees of increased apprehension. Many of the stories of attacks by marauding bands were placed after nightfall.

Lee had no difficulty getting up a force of armed men to stand watch on all sides of town. As he told himself, they wouldn't have been able to sleep anyway.

The following morning, an idea struck him as he was finishing breakfast on his way over to the jailhouse: someone should ride out to the wagon camps and spread the word about what had happened up at Aromanches, and might happen down in the Peralta country.

Because most of those stockmen were the same men who had been coming south for rich feed many years, most folks in town knew them. But Lee had met only one or two. One was young, on his first trip south. His father had died last winter. The other one was a grizzled, growly-voiced man named Henry Poole, who had been coming south forty years. He had told Lee, the first time they met up at Mike Kelly's place, about half a dozen hair-raising encounters he'd had with ragheads and renegade *bandoleros*.

Lee was at the jailhouse when a youthful rangeman tied up out front, walked in, and nodded as he said, "Mister Poole sent me to tell you some of our cattle was rustled last night." The youth looked for something to sit on, sank down, and spoke again. "The nighthawk heard 'em. At least he heard cattle movin' around when they should have been bedded down. He had a couple miles to cover. Anyway, by the time he figured out where the noise was comin' from, daylight was coming. He seen tracks, mostly cattle but with shod-horse sign behind them." The youth looked longingly at the coffeepot, so Lee told him to help himself, which he did, and returned to his bench with the cup.

"Mister Poole took the crew to run them bastards down an' sent me to tell you what's goin' on." The younger man sipped coffee, watching the marshal over the cup's rim. As he lowered it he said, "He don't think there'd be much call gettin' up a posse and scourin' around to find him. He said just to let you know there's rustlers in the country."

Lee leaned back, gazing at the cowboy, who was probably

older than he looked. Someone like Henry Poole wouldn't hire greenhorns. The youth was maybe seventeen, eighteen. He also guessed something else: Henry Poole was one of the old mossbacks, and he wouldn't want a lawman with deputized posse riders arriving while he was hanging rustlers.

"How many rustlers?" he asked.

"Four, accordin' to their sign. Mister Poole figures they're goin' to try an' make it down over the line with the cattle." For a moment the youth's eyes twinkled. "If I was a bettin' man, I'd lay ten to one they don't make it."

Lee did not say anything. Lynchings were against the law, but common.

He asked the youth to tell his employer the marshal would like to see him when he got back and could spare the time.

Lee returned to his desk with some coffee. He did not need some damned rustlers right now, and he was not even sure that if Henry Poole had sent the lad to get Lee to make up a posse and join in the run after the rustlers, he would have done it. Another time maybe, but not now.

There was one consolation. If Poole and his riders were pursuing rustlers toward Mexico, they would be far south of the probable route of marauders.

As for other cattlemen out yonder, he would send a rider to pass the warning.

CHAPTER THREE

The News!

CAP FRANKLIN WAS right. Excitement was not a sustainable emotion. After three days, town life returned pretty much to normal. The scouts from Mex-town returned having seen no marauders and not even any dust. The tragedy of Aromanches remained fresh, but of more immediate concern to the people of Peralta was the business of daily existence.

At the café, allusions to Aromanches became less as time passed, replaced by local gossip.

The marshal had sent a rider to warn outlying cattle camps of possible danger several days earlier. Since that time, several cowmen had ridden in out of curiosity; their riders, who ranged over miles of country, had seen nothing suspicious.

They did not disparage the marshal's warning. They, too, had heard of the Aromanches raid, but enough time had passed to convince them marauders had left the area.

Only one cowman did not appear in town. Henry Poole. Lee's curiosity increased as the days passed. It was possible the young rider Poole had sent in had neglected to inform his employer that the marshal wanted to see him.

But that was unlikely. Lee assumed Poole was too busy to make the ride to town. He wondered if Poole had caught the four rustlers and had brought his cattle back. Depending on how far he'd had to ride before catching them, he might not have gotten back for several days.

Lee thought he might ride out to Poole's camp, but was in no hurry. For one thing, he did not want to ride out there and find that the cattle had been recovered and that old Henry as well as his riders refused to discuss the matter, which would mean they had hanged the thieves.

Like most lawmen in isolated communities, adherence to book law was impossible for Lee Custis. He administered the variety of "natural" law that prevailed throughout the Southwest, and for a fact the military administrators of the Territory more often than not did the same.

He was down at Juan's cantina when the same attractive woman who had appeared earlier came to the doorway.

She handed an old man a note. As before, she ignored the marshal as she departed.

The old man gave the note to Juan, who read it and pushed it across the bar for Lee to read.

It was short and startling. *Arrieros* from Mexico had come upon three dead *gringos,* six dead cattle, and two dead horses, all shot to death. They had found a fourth *gringo,* a badly wounded older man hiding in a thornpin thicket. They had made a travois and were bringing him to Peralta.

Lee asked who the handsome woman was. Morales said her name was Lupe Villaverde and that she lived with her old grandfather in a little house with a large faggot corral behind it, south of the ruin of an old Spanish fort at the north end of Mex-town.

Lee kept the note and went looking for the house. He had no difficulty finding it. Lupe Villaverde was sweeping the *caliche* hardpan out front and stopped to lean on the broom as she saw him approaching.

The morning was not hot, but she had small beads of perspiration on her forehead. Behind her on a shaded small porch was a very old man wrapped in a blanket. His cheeks were sunken, his body was frail, blue veins showed in his hands, but his black eyes were bird-bright and direct. He watched the marshal approach his granddaughter to talk. He could hear nothing of what they said until she brought him to the shaded porch and offered him a bench. She then introduced him to the old man, speaking English.

"This is my grandfather. His name is Hernan' Villaverde. Grandfather, this man is the town marshal, Lee Custis."

They did not shake hands, but the old man smiled and nodded. He looked inquiringly at his granddaughter. This time she used Spanish.

"The note I showed you. He has it."

The old man's dark gaze swung to Lee. He knew very little English. He spoke Spanish, expecting Lupe to translate. When Lee answered in Spanish, he seemed pleased.

"I wanted to know how your granddaughter came by that message, and how long ago it was. If they are bringing the wounded man, I have to know about when they will reach Peralta."

The old man smiled and withdrew from the conversation by saying he had only glimpsed the rider with the note. All he could say was that he was an *arriero*.

Lupe explained further. "My father and brother had pack trains of mules. They traded both ways, down there and up here. They knew most of the Mexicans with pack trains. The *arriero* who brought the paper knew only where my brother lived, so he came here and gave me the note. Then he went back."

Lee asked about her father and brother. Her answer came after some hesitation. She glanced sideways at the old man before replying in English. "My father was killed six years ago by *guerilleros,* defeated revolutionaries fleeing from a Mexican route army. They needed his animals, so they shot him. My brother married a woman from Santa Fe and moved there."

Lee's gaze wandered. The area was quiet except for the intermittent shrieks of playing children.

He stood up and smiled at the woman. "I asked because it seemed odd to me that you would be given the message instead of—"

"I understand. I never saw the man before, but he told me he and my brother were very good friends."

"Did he know the name of the wounded man they're bringing to Peralta?"

"No. When he heard them he tried to crawl deeper into his thicket. When they found him he tried to shoot them, but his gun was empty."

"What'd he look like?"

"I'm sorry, I don't know." A faint smile came and went as she said, "He told me the old man could swear fiercely in Spanish and English. . . . I think they should reach Peralta by late afternoon."

Lee thanked her and was turning to depart when she spoke again. "He will need medicine and care. . . . *Señor,* my mother was a *curandera.* She taught me."

He smiled, nodded to the old man, and walked back to Juan Morales's cantina, which was empty except for the proprietor, who was painstakingly pouring the dregs from several cups and glasses into a large bottle.

Lee leaned on the bar and asked Juan, "Do you know an old freegrazer named Henry Poole?"

"Since I was a child, yes I know him. Everyone knows him. Is he the—"

"I don't know whether he's the wounded man or not. I do know rustlers ran off some of his cattle last week. They headed for the border. Henry and some of his riders went after them."

Juan did what he unconsciously did when he was upset:

he made a wide sweep of the bartop with a rag. "The cattle?"

"The *arrieros* said there were some dead ones down yonder, some dead horses and three dead gringos. I don't know about the other cattle."

Juan stared. "Henry Poole is an old man. He's been through Indian an' *bandolero* fights down here since I was a child. He wouldn't let himself be ambushed."

Lee shrugged. He, too, had thought of an ambush. It had to be some kind of surprise for him to be caught like that, and it was, but not for some time would people know what kind of an ambush it had been.

Lee returned to Gringo-town with the sun balancing atop some heat-hazed very distant mountains.

The news had preceded him. He'd barely fed the horses out back before he had visitors. The first one was Foggy Sommers, whose derby had a dent in the front of it that he had not taken time to punch out. He sat in a chair with his paunch well forward. His face had recently been washed; otherwise he looked as unkempt and dissolute as ever. "Henry Poole got shot up an' five of his riders was killed," he stated, looking straight at the town marshal.

"Three, not five, got killed. Henry—if it is Henry—will be along directly," he told the liveryman, who scratched his navel while digesting this information.

"They was sayin' up at the saloon Henry's so bad shot up he'll never get here alive. Damned border jumpers. Up at the saloon, men was sayin' we'd ought to round up everyone in town an' send for them cowmen on the range an' go down there, hang every *bandolero* we find an'—"

Lee blew out a noisy breath. "We're not going to do a damned thing until those Mex packers get here and we find out what those *arrieros* saw. Foggy, if it was border jumpers, by the time we could make up a posse an' get down there they'd be thirty miles into Mexico."

The liveryman straightened and stopped scratching.

"Let me tell you how it was done before you come here," he said, and Lee waved him into silence.

After the liveryman departed, Mike Kelly appeared without his bar apron and sweating like a stud horse. "I told you," he stated in an accusing voice. "I warned you over the bar, Lee. Border jumpers as sure as we're settin' here."

The marshal considered his friend. "How long have you known Henry Poole?"

"Well, he brought cattle down here long before I come here, an' I been here fifteen years."

The marshal continued to gaze steadily at Kelly. "Pretty savvy, was he?"

"Sure."

"Would he ride into an ambush?"

That stopped the saloonman. He eventually sank back and shook his head. "Not Henry Poole. Don't seem likely. Lee, I'd just about have to see it to believe it."

A lean, muscular young Mexican with sweat making large crescents at his armpits, with some of those little copper bells on his trousers and a face weathered shades darker than his normal color, pushed into the jailhouse with a hesitant demeanor.

Lee rose. So did Mike Kelly. The younger man rattled border Spanish in a quick, soft voice. "*Señores,* I am by name Raimondo Sanchez. We have put the wounded *gringo* at the cottage of my friend Villaverde." The young man shrugged. "We did not know of another place."

Kelly had to get back to the saloon. He had left it untended, expecting to be at the jailhouse only minutes. As he headed for his establishment, Lee gestured for the young Mexican to lead the way to Mex-town.

Mexican *arrieros* wore distinctive attire, different from other Mexicans', and they visited Peralta often enough to be identified on sight. That fact, plus the widespread knowledge that Mexican mule-train men were bringing the survivor of the southward battle to town, passed through Gringo-town like a sigh. By the time Lee and the Mexican reached the Villaverde house, people in Gringo-town were meeting in small groups, exchanging information, discussing courses of action. They possibly would have converged down in Mex-town if Mike Kelly hadn't yelled from out front of his saloon for them to stay out of Mex-town, to mind their own damned business.

Kelly's indignation had an effect, even upon those who normally would have challenged the saloonman; many thought Kelly's angry injunction was right.

For the time being, anyway, they would stay out of Mex-town.

A crowd did not gather in Mex-town, but for a different reason. The people down there were by long habit disinclined to become even distantly involved, particularly in anything that arose from violence.

Juan Morales was slumped dispiritedly in a chair on the tiny porch of the Villaverde residence. Overhead fronds provided some shade. He looked at Lee and jerked his head toward the door without saying a word.

There was no sign of the old grandfather. The house had four rooms; it was very large for Mex-town. The old man was sleeping like a stone in one of the rooms. His granddaughter appeared in a doorway, drying wet hands on a cloth. Her gaze was steady and unreadable. She gestured toward the room from which she had just emerged and spoke quietly in English. "He is in bed." When Lee started forward, she shook her head. "He is out of his head. Nothing he says makes sense. He mumbles about his mother and father back in Missouri . . . about someone named Beth he wanted to marry."

Lee tossed his hat on a chair and asked if she thought he would live. Her expression remained unreadable when she replied.

"Only if God is willing. He was shot four times. Two of those bullets could have killed him, and still may."

"It's Henry Poole?"

"Yes. Come to the kitchen with me for coffee." She walked past without looking back. He peeked into the room, which was so dark all he saw was a barely distinguishable face and the outline of a body under a cotton sheet.

In the kitchen, Lupe Villaverde filled two crockery cups from a pot atop a brick stove, motioned Lee toward the ancient, scarred-smooth old table, and sat opposite him regarding the coffee in her cup. He did not touch his cup, and waited.

When she raised her eyes she said, "I don't understand. . . . He was wounded down there for two days without water or care. His wounds are bad. Two should have killed him."

"He's a tough old man, Lupe."

Her eyes showed faint irony. "Even Saint John wasn't that tough, Marshal." She tasted the coffee before speaking again. "I've done everything I know to do. I don't see how he can live. I'm sorry. My father liked him. My grandfather, too, but my grandfather's memory is not very good anymore."

"Does he know who's in the room next to his?"

"No. He was carried in quietly. Juan Morales helped, then took the *arrieros* to his cantina. . . . Don't you like coffee?"

Lee looked down. He now had both hands around the cup. He raised it, drank, put it aside, and sighed. She regarded him, showing nothing in her face.

"I will tell you this," she said quietly. "I'll sit with him all night. Everything he needs or that can be done, I'll take care of. But . . . if he is alive in the morning it will be a miracle. Do you believe in miracles, Marshal?"

He rose, smiling crookedly at her. He knew nothing about miracles, had never witnessed one that he was aware of, and doubted there were such things. But he would have let wild horses drag him before he would have told her anything like that.

Her face was raised to him. She was stunningly beautiful; her expression was calmly composed. Obviously, she believed in miracles.

CHAPTER FOUR

Again!

AT JUAN'S CANTINA there were five Mexicans. The chief *arriero* was a tall, heavy man with a knife scar along the slant of his left jaw. He had challenging black eyes and a terse manner of speaking. While his younger companions stood in silence and Juan's usual quota of *viejos* listened, the leader leaned on the bar and explained in detail what he and his companions had found.

Several things interested the marshal. One was that shod-horse tracks indicated that the ambushers had been joined by three other riders who had arrived from the west, as though the point of the ambush had been previously agreed upon. Another interesting detail was that those shod-horse tracks had not continued southward toward the border after the attack, but had gone westward.

Of the cattle there was scattered sign. They clearly had been stampeded by fright when the gunfire commenced. Their tracks led in all directions.

The Mexican's final remark, delivered with a shrug of fleshy shoulders, was that the guns of the dead men had not been found. "The killers took those weapons with them—except for one gun beneath the body of a dead horse. It had not been fired."

An old man spoke while knocking dottle to the floor from his pipe. His first word was in Spanish, then he repeated it in English. "Ambush."

No one agreed or disagreed. The old man settled back on his bench, looking steadily at the large *arriero*.

The big man answered testily. "*Sí.*"

The old man said softly, "They took the guns and the horses. Why didn't they take the cattle?"

The heavyset *arriero* put a withering look on the old man, who responded by making a palms-down gesture with both hands as he spoke again in the same mild voice. "But, *jefe*, those were good beef cattle. Henry Poole had no other kind. Down in Mexico they would have brought a lot of money, and the border was close."

One of the younger *arrieros* made a statement that even his chief scowled about. He said, "The noise. They had to get away fast."

The old *mestizo* simply smiled at the younger man. No one stated the obvious: the attack had occurred a hundred miles from any town or habitation. The gunfire could have gone on all day and no one would have heard it.

Lee winked at Juan Morales and departed.

The points the old man had brought up bothered him, but he had little time to ponder. Two sweaty rangemen on hard-used horses arrived in town when the sun was high; left their horses with Foggy Sommers to be cooled out, rested, and fed; hiked up to the jailhouse; and burst in. The taller of the two said, "You know Johnny Alcorn?" to Lee Custis, who knew Alcorn only by name. He was the son of the cowman who had died the year before; he had followed his father's example of driving to the south desert each early spring.

"What about him?" Lee asked as the shorter of the sweaty men made a beeline for the *olla* and drank until fresh sweat burst out all over him.

The taller man, young but lined, bronzed, and hard-looking, sank onto a bench. "We ride for him. . . . We got hit last night by rustlers. They run off about sixty head, but this morning we found eight or ten that was left behind in the dark."

The shorter man returned to a bench, and while mopping off sweat, added more. "By daylight we seen their marks. Headin' straight south for the border."

Lee asked how many rustlers, and the short man replied while still mopping his face and neck. "Six sets of tracks."

"Shod horses?"

"Yeah. Our range boss's been comin' down here for ten years. He said it most likely wasn't Mex border jumpers, because they rarely ride shod horses."

Lee leaned back off his desk, regarding the rangemen. "Did Alcorn go after 'em?"

"John's been sickly the last few days. He wanted to, but the range boss told him about the rumor he'd picked up in town about Henry Poole. He told Johnny to send one or two riders to track 'em, but not to take us all because he figures them cow-stealin' sons of bitches know that south country like the palms of their hands and sure as hell they'd set up another ambush."

"So Alcorn sent a couple of trackers?"

"No, just one. A 'breed Indian named Johnny Gray Horse. He can track a fly across a glass window."

Lee was briefly silent. Trackers rode watching the ground. Gray Horse was probably not going to come back. Lee stood up. "On your way back go by Henry Poole's camp, tell his riders where he is and what happened to him and their friends. Tell them to rig out fully armed and come to town. Do the same with Alcorn. I'll get up a town posse. We'll wait here for you."

As the Alcorn riders stood up to depart, the taller one said, "Can't bring 'em all, Marshal. Mister Alcorn's been talkin' about stayin' close; we got a lot of critters out there."

Lee nodded. "Explain things to him. The more men we can get, the better."

He went up to the saloon, which was empty except for

some old gaffers playing toothpick poker near a corner window.

Mike Kelly watched the marshal cross the room and said, "You got a spry step for a warm day."

Lee leaned on the bar. "Do you know John Alcorn?"

"Well, I knew his father. I've only seen the young one a few times in town."

"He got raided last night the same way Henry Poole did. Only, they drove more cattle as they headed south."

Kelly did not get upset. "How is Henry this morning?" he asked.

Lee felt a twinge; he had not gone down to Mex-town to find out. Right now, with his mind finally made up to chase rustlers, he simply said, "I don't know, but last night that woman who's taking care of him didn't think he could last out the night."

Kelly was impassive as he said, "Lupe Villaverde? There aren't no secrets in Peralta. Do you know her?"

Lee was getting irritated. He replied a little sharply. "Mike, the cowmen are goin' to ride to town directly. I promised to get up a town posse. We're goin' to go after those sons of bitches."

Kelly went after two tepid beers, set one in front of the town marshal and nursed the other one. He was an almost imperturbable man, except when discussing politics; then he got profanely loud and opinionated.

"If they raided Alcorn's range last night, by now they're pretty darned far south. By the time you get up a posse and go after them, they'll be close to the border."

Lee did not dispute any of this. He said, "I need every man who owns guns an' can ride a horse. If we do nothing, by next week there'll have been more raids. . . . They killed three of Henry's riders."

"I know, an' you better be real careful. Those sons of bitches are sly as imps and ten times more deadly. They'll see your dust five miles before you get down there."

Lee said, "We're not going to make dust until after dark. Are you goin' to ride with us?"

Kelly nodded. "Sure. You want me to lock up an' go around town recruiting?"

Lee smiled for the first time since listening to the Alcorn riders. "You take the west side of the road an' I'll take the east side. We'll meet down at Foggy's barn an' wait for the rangemen."

Recruiting was not difficult. Even old Cap Franklin shed his apron, told his clerk where he was going, and headed home for his weapons and saddle animal.

Peralta, like most isolated communities that had been raided over the years (and even those that had not been, but were located in areas where marauders were known to pass through), had a vigilance committee made up of most of the town's able-bodied men. By the time Lee and the saloonman had gone around town, stores had been locked, horses were being cuffed and readied, men were examining weapons, making sure of their ammunition, and those with wives and families made their warlike preparations under the watchful eyes and white faces of their womenfolk.

Posse riding was not unusual in the Peralta country. This time the number of armed men preparing to leave town would set a precedent. This time, the women said among themselves, it was more like an army being raised to wage war, which had a very frightening effect.

As men riding or leading horses converged on the livery barn at the south end of town, Foggy was prepared to mount those who did not have horses. He was kept busy during the gradual increase out front until it seemed Peralta was being emptied of capable men, and horses.

Some old men shuffled up from their shacks to watch and to volunteer. Lee tried to be tactful. He recognized that while the spirit was willing, the bodies were unfit.

By midafternoon several of Henry Poole's riders reached

town. They went first to Mex-town to look in on their employer. Later, when they joined the increasing host of milling men and horses out front of the livery barn, they were particularly quiet and grim. They remained slightly apart from the noisy townsmen.

Mike Kelly had a big, jug-headed, pig-eyed, mule-nosed sorrel horse. He was naturally cranky. If another horse got too close, he would pin his ears back and lunge with his teeth.

Other rangemen rode in. Three were from Alcorn's outfit. Another group of five were from other cow camps, and while they were known to other rangemen, few were known to the townsmen, something that made no difference in the face of why they were there and where they were going.

One Alcorn rider approached Marshal Custis with a smiling expression on his face and a wary look in his dark eyes.

After introducing himself as Johnny Gray Horse, he told Lee he had tracked the rustlers and that they had lost a lot of cattle, which meant they were moving fast.

"Toward the border?"

"Yes. But they had a rider hangin' back watchin' for pursuit." The 'breed's eyes kindled. "Mexican with crossed shellbelts over his chest. He was *coyote*. Took me until the sun was slantin' away to catch him ridin' after his friends, past a thornpin thicket. I was afraid to shoot him, because I didn't know how far ahead his friends was. So I jumped my horse out of the thicket and hit his horse broadsides. It went down. It got up an' run like hell, but the Mexican was dazed. I cut his throat and brought his guns back to Mister Alcorn."

Lee gazed pensively at the 'breed. He was clearly satisfied that he had done right. When a riderless horse ran down to the other thieves, they would probably think pursuit was close.

Lee slapped the 'breed on the shoulder and went over where Cap Franklin was standing to repeat the story the 'breed had told him.

Cap was a calm, quiet man. "Can't be helped," he said, and looked stonily at the town marshal. "If it did anything, it scairt them enough so they'll ride hard for the border. . . . Marshal, I got a bad feeling about this mess. I'm going to stay in town."

Lee said nothing until everyone was ready to ride. Then he swung up and took the lead, with Mike Kelly at his side. Mike rode five yards before he twisted to look back at the following riders. As nearly as he could count, which was difficult with the riders all bunched up, there were sixteen of them.

Farther back, riding loosely and without haste, were seven more horsemen. Mike swore aloud. Lee twisted. Juan Morales was at the head of six heavily armed and well-mounted riders from Mex-town.

Mike said dryly, "Did you go down there?"

"No. Did you?"

Mike shrugged. It did not matter how the men from Mex-town had learned of the projected pursuit; every gun was welcome.

It was late enough in the afternoon to be hot when the possemen left Peralta. Mike Kelly drifted back to ride with the townsmen. There still was not much intermingling between rangemen and others. That would change over time, exactly as the distance between the others and the riders with Juan Morales would change. An odd thing about the prospect of danger was that it ameliorated barriers.

Juan eventually appeared beside Marshal Custis. He grinned widely. "I brought some friends. We want a shot at them Mexicans."

Lee stifled a laugh. Juan and his companions had been born north of the border, at Peralta. They occasionally rode down into Old Mexico, but despite common traditions and the language, did not consider themselves Mexicans. At least not Mexican-Mexicans. They were Mexican-Americans—discrimination, neglect, social disparagement notwithstanding.

Lee asked, "Did Henry Poole make it through the night?"

Juan sighed. "I didn't talk to Lupe, but I saw her as we left town. She was wearing black."

Daylight was fading when Johnny Gray Horse told Lee that while nightfall would hide them from sight, so many horses made noise. He was also of the opinion that the rustlers might have scouts on their back trail. Lee was inclined to agree.

The rangemen ate jerky and tinned sardines as they rode. The townsmen ate better, and the riders from Mextown had cold tortillas rolled around goat meat.

Water would become a problem. Johnny Gray Horse shook his head when Lee made an inquiry. He gestured with an upraised arm. The only water he knew of southward was not far from where the ambush had occurred. It was a little spring with two trees around it. But, he told Lee, there would not be enough water for all the horses and men unless Lee wanted to camp there long enough to allow the little spring time enough to recover each time it was drunk dry.

As the night advanced it got cooler, which was welcome. Gray Horse left the party for half an hour, to return and report that it was time they veered southwesterly, which was the route the rustlers had taken when he had caught and killed one of them.

The ground was sandy, which was fortunate, because otherwise the sound of more than twenty riders passing along probably could have been detected over a great distance. This was a still, empty, totally silent country. The farther they rode, the more stands of scrub brush they would encounter, along with nocturnal desert life such as runty brush rabbits, foraging owls, kangaroo rats with tails longer then their bodies, and both desert foxes and coyotes.

The little wind that had been a blessing hours earlier had long since died. Gray Horse rode slouched, chewing tobacco, something rare among Indians, but he was only one-quarter Indian. He had picked up other white-man vices, but as the result of having been nearly killed in a fight during which he had been drunk, he did not drink liquor.

CHAPTER FIVE

The Manhunt

THE TRACKING REPUTATION of Johnny Gray Horse was being put to the test. The night was not totally dark; there was a puny moon, a clear sky, and weak light from stars. Among the possemen, few thought the 'breed could accomplish what he undertook, which was simply to find the ambush site and pick up the trail to the west of it, and by walking ahead and leading his horse, to eventually also pick up sign of the second party of raiders.

These overlying tracks veered west exactly as did the underlying tracks. Johnny waited for the others to come up before giving it as his opinion that they were following the same rustlers who had committed the raid on Henry Poole and the Alcorn raid.

This surprised few possemen. Without a shred of proof, they had thought this might be the case long before reaching the ambush site; both raids had occurred in almost identical fashions.

Johnny Gray Horse walked ahead with his horse, closely watching the ground, moving slowly but steadily until he had covered about a mile and a half. Then he again halted to let his companions come close. He put a puzzled scowl on Marshal Custis.

"No cattle sign, Marshal. They keep goin' west. The border's maybe two hours straight south. Cattle thieves don't

33

go in the wrong direction, an' as far as I know, they don't lose cattle they risked their necks to steal."

For a long moment no one spoke. Then several men dismounted to spring their knees and rest their horses' backs, and one of them, a yardman for the Peralta way station, made a dry comment.

"After the fight with Henry Poole, maybe they had casualties. Maybe they figured more trouble was comin' an' let go the cattle an' skedaddled."

Juan Morales, leaning across the seat of his saddle, said, "Mexico is south, not west. Border jumpers would run for their native land, cattle or no cattle."

Mike Kelly and a man named Evans, who rode for one of the big range outfits, got into an argument.

Juan Morales got back astride in disgust and growled at Marshal Custis. "Keep on their trail. Sooner or later they'll most likely turn down toward the border."

But the tracks did not swing south. Johnny Gray Horse eventually tracked from the back of his horse because the sign did not change for several miles. It went west as straight as an arrow. To Lee Custis, this did not make a lick of sense—unless the rustlers weren't border jumpers, but were maybe some other variety of cattle thief, which was possible. Cattle rustling was a thriving avocation in areas close to the border.

Predicting the course of rustlers or, for that matter, other outlaws, reached a dead end whenever they did the unpredictable, causing confusion among pursuers and demoralizing them.

Particularly in territory where each posse rider was acutely conscious of the lack of water. Among the marshal's small army, one man with considerable experience told the others that unless they were chasing strangers to the south desert, which he did not believe was the case, those six murdering thieves knew where water was.

For this reason as much as because of the tracks, the possemen persevered.

Most of them had thought they would overtake the outlaws long before dawn. Now they were less sure, and this posed a serious problem: in daylight, riding slow or not, they would raise dust.

But it was still dark when Gray Horse halted, dismounted, and leaned above the tracks for a moment before straightening up, removing his hat to vigorously scratch as he turned to address the others.

"Turned north." As though expecting the others to doubt this, he faced forward and raised an arm. "See for yourselves."

Only two or three riders swung down to walk ahead. Again the 'breed pointed, then dropped his arm and swore. It did not make sense to him. The others went back to their animals and settled across leather in silence. It did not make sense to them either, but there was the sign.

Juan Morales walked along the northward tracks, leading his mount. He did not go far, maybe thirty yards, before remounting and riding back wagging his head. As a youth, he had ridden with posses after Indians. They were as tricky as coyotes. It had not been uncommon for them to leave a wide trail until they were far beyond any audible detection of gunfire, then circle around and come in behind their pursuers.

More than one posse army had taken heavy casualties as a result of those guerrilla tactics.

Juan sat among the others, hands atop the saddle horn as he said, "Either they aren't border jumpers or they're leaving tracks toward an ambush."

With the Henry Poole disaster fresh in mind, some of the townsmen showed obvious uneasiness. Lee sat near Juan Morales. He quietly suggested that Johnny Gray Horse take a couple of others with him and track the new route. Two of Poole's riders volunteered. The others sat their horses, watching the three ride northward.

Mike Kelly mentioned something Lee had thought of the first time he had ridden behind the Alcorn tracker. "If the sons of bitches are up there . . . we'll hear gunfire."

Lee told the men to dismount, which they did. They stood with their animals, looking northward where the three scouts were no longer visible.

They were losing time, which seemed not to occur to anyone.

The paling night grew colder. False dawn would appear shortly, to be followed by a rising sun.

An hour later, three silhouettes riding abreast appeared in the middle distance. Lee was relieved—and worried. He had expected a chase, maybe even a horse race; what he had not expected was bafflement.

Gray Horse drew rein and wagged his head. "Still goin' north. Two or three miles up there."

At least there had been no ambush. The company rode ahead again, with Gray Horse out front. Behind him Juan Morales came up beside the marshal, looking baffled. "Can't be border jumpers," he stated. Lee did not comment. By now probably none of the possemen still belived they were pursuing Mexican raiders.

The question was: who in the hell were they pursuing? Indians acted the way these outlaws were acting, but Indians neither rode shod horses nor had been active for some years.

Lee Custis kept his own counsel. He was never very talkative. The riders from Mex-town wondered among themselves if there wasn't an ambush up ahead.

Juan listened to this, found no fault with the reasoning, and loped ahead to explain to Lee what his Mex-town companions feared.

Their discussion was interrupted by the shrill neighing of a horse somewhere ahead. The noise did not last long enough for it to be pinpointed. The horse could be ten yards ahead or fifty yards.

Among the possemen someone snickered. "His friends'll kill him for letting his horse whinny."

Without speaking, Lee Custis swung to the ground with his Winchester. Eventually, all the possemen were dismounted with their saddle guns. Lee detailed four men to mind the horses.

He led the advance on foot, gesturing with one arm for the men to fan out as they advanced. His possemen got distance between each other as they moved ahead.

Ahead was a series of dense thickets, dusty, old, but evidently capable of flourishing in this environment. Among them were the ubiquitous thornpin bushes, safe even from starving animals. Their thorns were no less than two inches long, close-spaced and very sharp.

With a paling sky the possemen moved as close as they could get to cover, even among the thornpin bushes.

Once, some roosting wrens, roused by stalking men, made sleepy squeaks and fled. Another time a rodent-hunting rattlesnake halted, raised its head with lidless eyes, flicked its tongue, dropped low, and cranked its way furiously in a safe direction.

The horse whinnied again. This time the possemen could come close to placing the position of the animal. One rider, a dark, squatty man from Mex-town, stopped, leaned on his Winchester, and disgustedly spoke to Juan Morales. "A horsing mare. Would you ride a damned mare if you were an outlaw? I wouldn't. She smelled our horses."

He was right, but when the sour man scent reached her, she whirled and raced away.

The stalk ended a dozen yards ahead, where they found fresh droppings. The men scouted ahead another few yards in case it had not been a horsing wild mare, then slowly trudged back to their horses.

Very little was said.

Dawn was close. The sky was gray and cloudless, the air pungent with a scent of acidy plants.

Lee and Mike conferred at length. As they were doing this, Juan Morales and a companion loped around the dense scattering of underbrush and up a low roll of land. They sat up there in plain sight.

Kelly's opinion was offered as a set of alternatives. Without water they could probably get through the oncoming day, but if they rode down the outlaws and there was much of a fight, by evening they would be riding suffering animals, and they were at least fifty miles from Peralta, their only known source of water.

Or they could give up and turn back. The listening men waited for the marshal to make the decision, but from their tired, beard-stubbled faces it was not difficult to decide which course most of them preferred.

Juan Morales and his companion came racing back from their position atop the low land swell. Their ride attracted everyone's attention. Before they reached the others, Juan yelled something in Spanish and swung his arms.

The discussion between the marshal and saloonman was forgotten.

Juan hauled down to a sliding halt that threw dust as he said, "About three miles northward there is a spiral of smoke from a cooking fire. There are some men crouched around it."

The implication was exactly what the possemen wanted to believe: they had finally found their outlaws.

Without a word, they got astride and followed Juan. Johnny Gray Horse rode wide to skirt around the land swell.

Lee held up his hand to slacken the pace of his possemen. Now there was no longer a sign of demoralization or worry. Every rider had unshipped his carbine. Some held them across their laps; others held them upright, butt plate against a leg.

They halted behind the land swell, invisible to the men far ahead around their fire. No one doubted that the outlaws were cooking their first meal of the day. The possemen looked contemptuous; only idiots would sit down calmly, light a smoking fire, and prepare breakfast without detailing at least one man to seek a high place to keep watch. Particularly when they thought they might be the object of a manhunt.

Lee impatiently waited for Gray Horse to return, which he did at a steady walk. When he reached the others he said simply, "Six of them. We been following six tracks. There's no sign of anyone else as far as I can see. And them tracks go straight toward that fire."

Lee waited a moment, looked around where men with weapons in hand looked back, as ready as they would ever be.

It was a fair distance, about two miles from the land swell. The outlaws would see them and scramble for their horses. After that it would be a horse race.

Lee nodded and eased his horse to the left, around the base of the land swell. Half the riders followed him and half followed Juan Morales, who was riding around the east side of the mound.

Once they were in flat, more or less open country, there was no reason not to run their animals. They were not seen for a couple of minutes, riding like the wind, fanning out and raising dust.

They covered the first mile and were starting to get closer when the men ahead jumped up, ran for their horses, and sprang astride. One man halted to aim and fire. His horse fidgeted; the bullet went wild. He plunged the Winchester into its boot and raced after his companions, who were well ahead and aiming toward a distant boulder field to the northeast.

CHAPTER SIX

Strangers

DAWN REVEALED A veil-like high overcast. In other places this usually meant rain was on the way, but in New Mexico's Middle Domain it rarely rained after February, except for a few warm sprinkles, barely enough to settle dust.

People in Peralta were relieved when they arose to find high clouds were filtering some of the sun's heat. It was likely the sunlight would burn through by midafternoon.

For the mourners in Mex-town, the cool morning was a blessing, as they slowly proceeded to the old burial ground where the ruins of the Spanish fort stood. Their somber mood was enhanced by the still, gray overcast. Lifelessness seemed to permeate their surroundings.

Ahead, several elderly men wheeled Hernan' Villaverde's crude wooden coffin atop a two-wheeled cart. Directly behind them walked Lupe Villaverde and several older women. The sickly old man had died in his sleep.

There were tears farther back in the shuffling crowd of mourners, mostly women, but neither Lupe nor the women with her showed emotion. They were dry-eyed, resignedly solemn.

The open grave with mounded earth on both sides was deep enough to require several of the men to rig the coffin to be lowered with ropes.

Because Peralta's resident priest had been withdrawn some time earlier, a frail elder, dark and wrinkled as an-

cient leather, pulled off his hat to recite from the Bible by
memory.

Lupe trickled moist earth over the hole. She was followed by others. An old man broke down and cried behind
his upheld hat.

The gravediggers leaned to their work with shovels on
each side of the hole. Listening to the measured shovelfuls
of dirt being dropped on wood served to remind mourners
how fleeting life was, how inevitable was death.

Mourners turned and slowly started back. Suddenly they
heard wood being violently smashed from the direction of
the empty plaza. They hurried to the plaza, but they saw
no one. As they began to disperse toward their residences,
two dusty, unkempt *bandoleros* rode lean horses toward the
well, at a slow walk.

They stopped in front of the well, across the plaza from
the people. The *bandoleros* were shaggy, unshaven men
with machetes slung from their saddles, as well as booted
carbines and laden shellbelts from which were suspended
Colt revolvers in cutaway holsters.

Most women moved hastily indoors. There was a period
of deathly quiet. The men in the center of the plaza
seemed to be waiting for something. Dozens of eyes
watched from secret places. Children were called in
hushed voices to come inside.

There was a wide alley separating Mex-town from
Gringo-town, with the rears of stores across the alley. Business establishments in Gringo-town faced the roadway.
There were several dogtrots between the buildings lining
the roadway in Gringo-town, but whites wishing to visit
Mex-town had to go to either the north end of Peralta or
the south end, where there were crossroads.

After Mexico lost her farthest provinces to the North
Americans, when settlers, mostly merchants, had come to
settle, they invariably ignored villages already in existence
to build their own parts of town with their backs to the

plazas, *jacals*, and dusty, crooked byways of the old towns, a condition that pleased as many natives as it did *gringos*. Each had a particular way of life.

This situation had one noticeable problem, but it, too, was accepted without a murmur: people in Gringo-town could not see what was transpiring in Mex-town, and vice versa. At the beginning, the residents of both parts of Peralta found no fault with this arrangement, although there had been times when the separation worked against the common good of Peralta.

The motionless horsemen out in the plaza waited, rarely seemed to converse, studied Mex-town with the indifference of men who had seen dozens of such south desert communities.

In Gringo-town, six unkempt riders appeared with the sun at their backs, walking their horses, saying nothing among themselves. One wore crossed bandoliers; the others, although bronzed from exposure, were *gringos*. Heavily armed, they rode in the middle of the road.

People who saw them reacted as instinctively as the people had in Mex-town. They stepped into stores, went briskly to their homes, herding youngsters ahead. The few men in Gringo-town who paused to stare were mostly old or troubled by crippling infirmities. A tall, thin old man with a wooden leg from the knee down stepped into the recessed doorway of the general store to watch the oncoming riders. He had lost his lower leg to a cannonball at Antietam.

Among the strangers was a rawboned, vicious-looking man with matted fair hair. Frank Bauman had bold eyes, a scar on one cheek, and a bloodless slit for a mouth. He rode half the distance, saw the one-legged man watching from the recessed doorway, drew, and fired.

The one-legged man was slammed backward under the impact. He tried to turn, to twist, but died on his feet and fell forward across the plankwalk, leaking blood from his mouth.

In Mex-town, the pair of riders in the plaza passed a few words back and forth, reined across in the direction of the nearest houses, and as a ten-year-old boy stepped forth to stare, one of them shot him through the head. The other horseman saw a woman fleeing for shelter and shot her through the back.

The gunshot in Gringo-town had evidently been a signal. Other riders appeared in both Mex-town and Gringo-town. They went among the residences and stores shooting. They killed an old man who had wanted to ride with the possemen. A stray dog was shot three times and fell dead in roadway dust. Two horsemen rode across his carcass in the direction of Mike Kelly's saloon, where one man reined his horse in close and shot the big lock off the doors. But none of them dismounted to enter; they turned around to join their companions, looking for targets.

Peralta's midwife was peering past the partially opened door of her small house. Two men called to each other, making a bet. First one fired, then the second one fired. Both bullets passed through the door about where the shooters had guessed her body would be. One bullet shattered the door, struck a steel hinge, and sang off into space. The second bullet hit the midwife under her right arm and exited on the opposite side. She fell dead against the door.

Several riders went around at the south end of Gringo-town to join their friends in Mex-town. They smashed the wooden door of Morales's cantina. They tied their horses and walked into the cool gloom. They broke bottles, smashed benches and chairs. Then they each took two bottles, one in each hand, one for immediate use, one for their saddlebags.

Intermittent gunfire continued until midday. At one

point it became fierce, as three men who had been unable
to ride with the marshal forted up in the blacksmith shop.

This was the kind of sport the killers enjoyed. Bauman
and his men tied their animals, stalked around on all sides
of the smithy, drawing fire from a nervous defender, then
stood up and blasted the entire building.

Inside where anvils stood, bullets sang in all directions.
One defender died screaming as a lopsided ricochet tore
through his body about belt-high and emerged in frag-
ments past his right shoulder blade.

Parched, warped wooden siding broke and splintered;
hanging tools flew in all directions. The two survivors were
busy ducking and dodging; their firing became erratic.

The fight ended when Bauman yelled and ran straight
at the broken-wide roadway door. His companions also
shouted and ran forward. Firing was incessant and thun-
derous.

Bauman sprang past a sagging door and shot a man in
the face who was turning in terror. One man still fought.
He was behind a wheelwright's big quenching tub. He fired
at the leader, missed by a foot, cocked his handgun to fire,
pinched the trigger. Nothing happened. The gun was
empty.

Bauman walked directly toward the quenching vat and
shot the defenseless man through the neck.

In the roadway there were no longer any targets. Bauman and the others milled, yelling back and forth, then
loped to the south end of town and turned around. They
reloaded with reins between their teeth, and when Bauman spurred his animal, the others did the same. They
raced the full length of Gringo-town, firing randomly.
Glass broke, wood shattered, signs and doors were riddled.
This charge did the least actual harm yet. By the time it
ended, Peralta's residents were hiding, shaking with fear.
The town was cowed. Those with arms, and still willing to
fight, did almost nothing. They had seen what happened

to resisters. Also, without a prayer of the kind of support they would need, prudence suggested waiting to fight another day.

The gunmen left three men outside the saloon while they looted Kelly's place exactly as others had done in Mex-town. They went behind the bar using carbines to sweep dozens of bottles to the floor, to fling others through windows, and to finally rest from their hour-long slaughter with whiskey. None of them pumped beer into glasses or tin cups. They drank whiskey.

Over in Mex-town only two men remained, the original duo who had sat near the well. These two did not join their companions in Gringo-town, nor did they spur their animals or make gunfire charges. They passed back and forth among the *chozas*, cocked guns in hand, prepared to kill, but only if they were denied what they sought.

Curiosity led a young woman to try to get a closer look at them. Her leg had been broken during childhood and improperly set, so that while she could walk, she had a definite limp.

A squatty, burly *bandolero* saw her, whipped his horse around, and jumped it out as the crippled girl screamed and ran. Even without a limp, she stood no chance against a horse.

The *bandolero* swooped low, caught a fistful of hair, and upended her as though he were upending a steer by the tail.

The breath was knocked out of her, but she fought back as the horseman stepped down and lunged at her. She scrambled clear of the groping hands until she regained her feet and ran blindly.

He caught her near the adobe house of Lupe Villaverde. When she twisted in his grip and beat him with two small fists, the *bandolero* laughed, tightened his grip, and moved to fling her to the ground. She was still writhing and screaming when two guns sounded almost simultaneously.

The man flung up both arms, freeing the crippled girl, who did not look back until she was almost breathless from running.

The *bandolero* lay sprawled on his face.

His companion came around the side of the house, saw the dead man, saw the distant girl, whirled his horse, and rode swiftly toward the north end of Mex-town to reach Gringo-town and return with his friends.

A dozen pair of eyes had watched this affair from hiding. Only one person walked out into plain sight, a small, dark woman with fury on her face. Marta was carrying a hexagonal-barreled Winchester rifle.

She called to the girl and gestured. The girl fled.

Marta raised her gaze to the front of the Villaverde house where a fading tendril of soiled gunsmoke was diminishing under the overhang. She crossed to the door and called in Spanish. When Lupe opened the door, she was still holding the big old cap-and-ball pistol that had belonged first to her grandfather, then to her father.

Marta made no move to enter. She said, "I'm going out to light the greasewood pile."

Lupe reached, pulled her inside, barred the door, and said, "How? They are everywhere; it is open country all the way out there. Marta, it's still daylight."

Marta said, "I had no idea you were watching what was happening to the girl."

Lupe put the heavy old gun aside. "She screamed loud enough. Everyone must have heard." Then she looked at the long rifle with the hexagonal barrel and said, "Doesn't it kick?"

"Like a mule. Should we hide the body?"

Lupe sank limply onto a bench. "Why? His friend saw him lying dead. He ran for help. They'll come soon."

Lupe's gaze was about equal parts resigned and desperate.

Marta rallied and said, "We can get others. We *have* to

get others," and moved toward the door. As she passed she gave Lupe a light shove. "Go out the back way. Tell everyone you find that unless we fight they are going to kill us all." The short woman's eyes brightened with harsh irony. "They are going to kill us all anyway—but we don't have to make it easy for them."

Marta opened the door, listened to the deathly silence, saw nothing threatening, and went swiftly toward her own residence. She was not there long. She went among other residences, pounding on doors, calling through glassless windows, answering whispered questions, moving quickly.

Lupe Villaverde sat a long time before also going among the other residences. She was less strident, but as desperate as Marta. Several men opened doors to her. She passed her message and refused to come inside for shelter.

In Gringo-town, Bauman and his men had nearly demolished Kelly's saloon. He took several men aside with instructions to go among the houses and find hostages, preferably women and children. After these men departed he returned to the bar, beat atop it with his pistol barrel until most of the racket died. He turned and told his companions they should make a fire in the iron stove, leave the door open, and find iron rods.

He did not say more. He did not have to. This phase of the attack had been gone through many times. It was infallible, and it saved the time searching for money and valuables would require.

Bauman said they should finish with Peralta before sundown, fire it and leave, something his men accepted, because this was the way they had successfully operated many times. As he finished speaking, a bandit named Jose burst past the broken doors to say Pedro Aguirre had been shot and killed down in Mex-town while trying to catch a girl.

Yells of anger erupted and men headed for the door. Some were unsteady from drinking as they left the saloon and mounted their horses.

One man, a bitter-faced individual with thinning hair beneath a greasy hat, stopped, aimed, and fired at the jail-house. The sound of a bullet striking a three-foot-thick adobe wall was lost among the other noises as men got astride and drew handguns. They were wheeling north-ward when someone farther south fired from hiding. Bau-man yelled for the riders to follow him. He turned south-ward toward the house closest to Aguirre's body. As the riders rode past, each man fired into the little house where the sniper must have hidden. There was no return fire.

The attack in Mex-town was suddenly halted by sounds of intense gunfire in Gringo-town. It made the air rever-berate. Bauman yelled and wheeled to lead the rush out of Mex-town at the lower end and back into Gringo-town.

All but two of Bauman's raiders had charged over to Mex-town to avenge the killing of Pedro Aguirre. Only the men sent to find hostages were left behind. They had run into armed resistance when they approached the livery barn.

CHAPTER SEVEN

The Siege

IN MEX-TOWN, THE withdrawal of the raiders and the subsequent sounds of a fierce fight at the lower end of Gringo-town offered a respite. Marta appeared at the house of Lupe Villaverde still carrying her heavy old rifle. She said the survivors were gathering at Morales's cantina. She had already told others to hasten there with all the weapons and ammunition they could find.

Lupe told her that Poole was too weak to make it to the cantina. Marta ran outside and beckoned to four hurrying women. With three women supporting each side, they carried Poole's bed to the cantina. The occupied bed was placed against the wall.

There were fourteen women and three men, everyone armed with at least one weapon. Some also had machetes. There was fear, pure terror, but with little time for it, no panic.

Four old grandmothers had rounded up all the children and taken them to a musty, damp, dark hole beneath the old Spanish fort. They hid with the children down there in pitch darkness. The hole had once been a military guardhouse for recalcitrant soldiers and other prisoners.

They could hear nothing.

At the cantina, frightened people listened to the savage battle at the lower end of Gringo-town. Marta leaned aside her heavy old gun and told the others they could fight only as long as their ammunition lasted. She also reminded them very vividly what would happen to them if the raiders got inside the cantina. She placed the three men—two were old, one had a humped back—to keep watch at the glassless window, then barred what remained of the shattered door with chairs and benches.

An older woman grinned at Marta and said, "*Lo Alamo.*" It *was* like the Alamo.

Several women found two brooms and cleared broken bottles from the slippery floor. They worked as though this was what they needed to do in order not to think.

Lupe hovered near Poole's bed. He was conscious, had understood for an hour or more what was happening, but said nothing. Only his eyes moved.

When two young women leaned to peek past the window, he growled. Lupe called over the babble of voices for the young women to get away from the window.

The humpbacked man standing guard over there looked around, saw the bedridden older man's scowl, and winked.

The battle at the lower end of Peralta gradually diminished and eventually stopped altogether.

Bauman and his men approached the riddled livery barn with caution. They found the two who had been detailed to take hostages. One was dead; the other was wounded, but had managed to kill the armed liveryman. Frank Bauman ordered his men to return to the saloon.

Once inside, Bauman took two swallows from a bottle and shoved it along Kelly's bar, where other hands reached for it. He was in a foul mood. They had struck as they always tried to do, with the sun at their backs. They had indiscriminately killed people to terrify the town, and that, too, had proceeded as it usually did. But for over an hour now they had been delayed by acts of resistance. This was taking too much time.

Jake Bentley, a bitter-faced graying killer, wiped his lips

and said, "We got to get hostages; otherwise we're goin' to be wastin' more time tryin' to find valuables."

Bauman agreed. He sent Jake with four men to apprehend and return with women and children. If they encountered any men, they were to kill them on sight.

The day was nearly spent. The rest of the raiders drank and waited; some strolled in pairs on either side of the roadway, guns in hand. After the fight at the livery barn, there was not a breathing thing in sight. Occasionally the half-drunk renegades would fire through a window, or in other ways try to flush someone out to run so they would have moving targets.

Peralta was a ravished, corpse-littered town. To all appearances, it was as dead as the bodies in the roadway and behind doors.

Jake and one of the men found a woman, but she heard them in the alley and ran for her house. They went after her, reached the door too late, and fired two rounds at the lock. The door swung inward.

The woman was too frightened to do more than stand with her back to a small table, hands braced behind her.

Jake told the woman to get away from the little table. She obeyed stiffly. From the opposite side of the room, darkened as much by oncoming dusk as from closed shutters, a gangling youth appeared.

He froze.

Jake's partner moved his eyes slowly from the slim woman to the doorway. He and the startled youth exchanged looks. The young renegade jerked his head. "Get over by your sister," he said.

The youth started to obey as he said, "She ain't my sister, she's my mother."

Jake asked who else was in the house. The woman couldn't speak. Her son said, "No one. Paw's out with the posse."

Jake's expression changed slightly. He seemed about to

laugh, but instead he said, "Well, now, you got any idea when he'll be back? I'll tell you—not until hell freezes over." He jerked his head. "Out the front door. Slow, folks. Real slow."

Outside, Jake, aware of the look on his companion's face as he stared at the woman, growled softly. "I'll take these to the saloon. You see what else you can find."

The sullen-faced man started to protest, but the graying man held up a stiff finger. The younger renegade walked away with murder in his eyes.

Jake had almost reached the saloon when he heard a gunshot from across the road southward, the direction his companion had taken. He shrugged, shoved the woman through the doorway, and punched her son into the saloon as well. The loafing renegades inside turned and became very quiet.

Frank Bauman turned to look at the first hostages while turning a red-hot rod in the glowing belly of the stove.

The woman was glassy-eyed with terror. Her son moved stiffly at her side. One of the renegades, drunker than the others, spat, wiped both hands down the outside of his filthy trousers, and started forward with a leering smile.

Bauman snarled at him. "Grant, gawddamn you, leave her be until she's told us a few things."

The drunken man turned on Bauman without his smile. "Then what?" he growled.

Bauman was turning the red-hot rod when he replied offhandedly, "Then you can have her. Now get back to the bar."

Grant moved back, but his gaze never left the woman.

Bauman told another outlaw, "Fetch a chair, Bert. Take off her shoes an' stockings."

The short man obeyed without showing any expression. As he pushed the woman down on the chair, her gangling son cried out and ran forward. A lantern-jawed man shoved out his foot to trip the youth. Then he struck the boy on the back of the head with a gun barrel, and this time when the youth fell he did not move. Blood colored his hair crimson.

The woman fainted.

Frank Bauman removed the hot iron, spat on it, listened to its sizzle, and turned to put an annoyed look at the woman, who would have slumped off the chair but for the restraining hand of the short man who had removed her shoes and stockings.

It bothered him that this whole damned business was taking too long. He took consolation from the way he had drawn the able-bodied possemen away from Peralta, but every delay, such as this one with the woman who had fainted, bothered him.

He told several men to go find more hostages. After these men departed, he placed the iron back in the stove, got a bucket of greasy water from behind the bar, and flung it full force into the woman's face.

She recoiled and sputtered, but recovered consciousness very slowly. Her son was lying facedown in a pool of blood. She screamed and tried to rise swiftly. The short man behind her pulled her roughly back down and held her in the chair by both shoulders.

She moaned and rocked slightly from side to side. A lean, vicious-looking man with an ivory-handled six-gun on his left side said, "For Chrissake, Frank, we're goin' to be here after dark."

That had a sobering effect even on the men who had been drinking. So far this outlaw band had never remained in a village after sundown, for the very excellent reason that other bands, with rare exceptions, who had survived dark nights in attacked towns had too few men left by morning to continue raiding as a group.

Bauman glared at the speaker, but the remaining renegades looked stonily at him. These were two-legged wolves who operated like any other killer pack; when a leader made a serious mistake, they tore him to pieces.

Their attention was diverted, because two men brought in more women, young and attractive.

One of the two raiders, a man named Cody, shoved the trembling women ahead and grinned at his companions around the room. "They didn't tell me their names. This here little one with the black hair and the big breasts—she was sucklin' a baby when I walked in. Her husband drives stage. He's up north at that town we raided a week or so back. Won't return for a couple days."

The lantern-jawed man roughly shoved both women toward the center of the refuse-littered, whiskey-smelling room.

Not a sound was made until the seated woman began to moan as she rocked on her chair. The two latest hostages stared as though they would faint. One did, in fact, begin to reel, but a man behind them caught her by the hair; the pain of his yanking put her mind on something more personal and immediate.

Bauman removed the glowing poker from the stove and gestured with it for the moaning woman to be shoved off the chair and for the young mother to be pushed down in her place.

The moaning woman crawled on all fours to the side of her unconscious son, raised his bloody, swollen head to her lap, and rocked slightly as she wiped dirt and blood off his face.

A renegade filled his glass with beer, crossed over, and flung the beer in the lad's face. His mother crouched to protect him, too late. Her moaning began and continued until Bauman threatened her with the glowing poker; then her wounded-animal sounds ceased.

He turned to the woman in the chair, held the glowing poker within a foot of her face, and said, "You're goin' out of here blind unless you tell me where every bit of gold, jewelry, and money is cached."

The woman looked past the hot iron, squinting from the heat, and replied in a surprisingly calm, steady voice. "I can't tell you where it all is. I doubt if anyone can. Folks don't advertise where they hide money and such like. All I can tell you is where the wife of the man who runs the stage office in town, an' me an' my husband, got our savings."

"How do you know where the stager's wife's got her cache?"

"Because she's my mother."

A renegade speaking in a slurred voice asked if Bauman wanted him to fetch in the woman's mother. He thought she might know more than her daughter knew about hidden wealth.

Before Bauman could reply, the woman swung her attention to the man at the bar and said, "I'd sure like you to go to her. My mother died two weeks ago."

For five seconds only the sound of cooling coals was audible, then the graying man laughed, eyed the big-breasted woman with a faintly kindling respect, and turned to reach for a bottle atop the bar as others also laughed.

CHAPTER EIGHT

"Quien es?"

FOR THE PEOPLE inside Morales's cantina, waiting was terrible. They had faintly heard a woman scream. They had also heard several gunshots.

The humpbacked man watched dusk settle with probing eyes. Right at this moment, all he wanted from life was a clear target.

Lupe Villaverde hovered beside Poole's bed.

Marta came to her. "Whatever they are doing," she said, believing she and every other woman in the cantina knew what the renegades were doing in Gringo-town, "we can't stay in here forever. I am going to try and set fire to the greasewood west of town."

Lupe stared. Even assuming settling dusk and oncoming night would provide protection, the pile of wood was half a mile from town. Even if Marta could reach it, start it burning, her chance of returning safely was slight. Marauding bands understood the purpose of those flaming beacons.

Lupe said softly, "No! We can hold out until the men return."

Marta pointed in silence to a shattered *olla* that had held the only water.

Lupe made a desperate suggestion. "The men may already be coming. All that gunfire—"

"They would have arrived by now," Marta said. She

56

shrugged. "If they tire of whatever they're doing in Gringo-town and come back down here—be careful with ammunition. It is dark. Let them get very close first." Marta placed a small hand lightly on Lupe's arm and smiled, turned toward the door where the humpback and another man were squinting. She touched them. Every eye in the cantina was on her as she eased the men aside, moved chairs and benches, and splintered wood until she could crawl through. A man hissed and held out his old six-gun. She took it, eased out, told them to block the door after her, and went swiftly northward in the direction of the nearest *jacals*. Someone's thirsty goats bleated as she slipped past.

Without a belt, she had to carry the old Colt in her hand. The total silence was eerie. Marta had lived here all her life. This was the first time she had hurried past the residences when someone did not call a soft greeting. Normally at this time, children played, fought, and cried, and whole families sat in the cool late evening on tiny porches.

Dusk had yielded to nightfall. Stars became brighter; there would be no moon for some time yet. She moved swiftly, rarely halted to listen, reached the northernmost part of Mex-town where the eroded mud fort stood, and without hesitation turned to her left. She walked soundlessly but briskly in a half-horseshoe course that would take her up and around Gringo-town and across the north-south roadway several hundred yards above town.

There were lights in Gringo-town. Not many; the brightest came from the saloon. She could hear loud voices and, once, a scream of raw terror. She wanted to run. She also wanted to sneak southward, take a position across from Kelly's building, wait until a renegade walked out and kill him.

She crossed the roadway, saw and heard nothing ahead, and was beginning to increase her pace when a man arose out of the ground thirty feet ahead. He aimed his handgun and cocked it. Marta dropped like a stone. The dark shadow did not fire; instead he said, "Dolores . . . ?"

Marta could hardly speak. "No. Who are you?"

The man's gun arm sagged. *"Quien es?"*

"Marta Sandoval."

The man stood in silence for a moment, then let his breath out in a ragged sigh. He said in Spanish, "I almost shot you."

Marta rose. "Who are you?"

"Wes Coleman, a yardman for the stage company. . . . What are you doing out here?"

She knew the yardman, not well but well enough. He had married the daughter of Pio Alvarado six years earlier. They had three children. She asked where his family was. He sank to his haunches as he replied, "They're hiding at the corral yard in the hay. What are you doing out here?"

"I'm going to fire the beacon."

He nodded. "That's what I was fixin' to do when I backgrounded you." He rose. "Come along."

As they moved together, she asked about the renegades. His reply chilled her blood. She told him the women would be fools not to lead the raiders to everything of value in Peralta. He said nothing until they could distantly make out the pile of greasewood, then he stopped, brushed her arm lightly, and without a word sank to the ground.

She had not seen or heard anything, but she took cover beside him. Then she heard horses walking. She leaned to whisper that it must be the returning possemen. He held up a finger for silence.

She saw two slow-pacing shadows as they emerged from the night. If they were possemen, there should be many more. If they were not possemen, who were they? She looked at the yardman. He ignored her to watch the pair of horsemen.

If they were strangers and rode into Peralta now, they would be killed by the first raider who saw them. If they were part of the renegade band . . . She was raising her six-gun when the man beside her reached and very slowly forced her arm to the ground. He almost imperceptibly shook his head.

She did not try to raise the gun again.

The pair of horsemen abruptly halted as unmistakable screams and laughter echoed through the night. They sat for a long time listening. Eventually one rider said, "They're here, Elam! The sons of bitches are here!"

His companion did not argue. When he spoke, his voice had an overlay of bafflement. "In the night, for Chrissake? It can't be Bauman. He never stays after sundown."

The first man was skeptical of that. "Not until now, but you seen the tracks, the camp, the sign of them ridin' in this direction. . . . Come along, we got to get back, fast."

Marta and Coleman were motionless as they watched the strangers turn and boot their horses into a lope. They speculated that the horsemen hadn't been renegades; they had sounded more like army scouts or maybe riders from another ravaged settlement trailing the marauders.

Coleman sat up, listening to diminishing sounds as he said, "Bauman? Is that the name they used?"

"Yes."

"Do you know who Frank Bauman is, Marta?"

She had no idea.

"It was Bauman's band that nearly wiped out Aromanches up north. One of our drivers came back with that information. He's said to be the worst marauder between here an' Texas."

Marta half heard; she was alternately listening to the fading sounds of the riders and straining to see the pile of greasewood.

They stood up and strode in the direction of the greasewood pile. As they approached the pile, Coleman paused for a long time, looking and listening. It was no longer possible to hear noise from town. Everything out here was peacefully silent and faintly flower-scented.

While Marta fished for her *fosforos*, Coleman held up a hand. Marta waited until he lowered it, then nodded and dropped to her knees. She lighted a wildly flashing, fiercely smoking sulfur match, shielded its brilliance with her body, and put the fire into a nest of dry chips.

The fire caught immediately. Coleman grabbed Marta's arm, pulled her upright, and said, "Run!"

It was sound advice. The greasewood, which had been out there for several years, was as dry as tinder. Within moments flames were licking from the bottom toward the top.

By the time Marta and Coleman were a hundred yards easterly, the entire pile was brightening the night with light that could be seen for miles. It could also be readily seen from Peralta, and its brilliance highlighted a pair of running people, one short, one tall.

Marta and Coleman had to slacken pace to catch their wind. The yardman dropped flat. Marta followed his example.

They rose and continued running, got almost within sight of the stage road when a wild howl sounded from the upper end of Gringo-town.

The runners were pumping air like a bellows, but did not stop after that yell. They reached the road, crossed it, and the yardman said this was as far as he could go with Marta. He turned southward in the direction of town.

Marta watched him go, wondering whether he would reach the corral yard and the hay pile before the renegades boiled out of the saloon like ants, scattering in all directions.

She got back to Mex-town, sweaty and with a pounding heart, but feeling exultant about having accomplished her purpose as well as having gotten back without being detected—and almost ran into the open arms of the burly *bandolero* who had been going from house to house stealing whatever was valuable. He had a sack tied to his waist on one side, a large knife on the other side.

He probably had not as yet seen the beacon fire. He was as surprised as she was. He was also less quick-witted. She ducked and dodged, but he ran well, yelling to her why he wanted her to stop and what they would do when he caught her.

With burning lungs and a heart threatening to tear free of its cage, she went behind a one-room *jacal*, flattened against the rough wall, and raised her six-gun.

The renegade did not appear.

She waited and tasted real fear. Her pursuer was smart; he was not going to charge around a blind corner.

The next-nearest residence was the home of Lupe Villaverde. It was about twenty yards, too far.

Her palm was sweat-slippery around the six-gun; the only sound was her own breathing. She was certain he could hear it.

A harsh laugh sounded on her right from the corner opposite the one she was watching. Before she could turn and raise the gun, the man ducked behind the house.

Marta inched along the wall in the direction the man had taken. When next he came around to turn her blood cold with his laugh, she would be waiting.

It was another long wait. This time he did not laugh from either corner of the house. He was moving soundlessly to get between Marta and the cantina. He was experienced in the game of cat and mouse.

He could have shot her several times. Nerves taut, her throat dry, she had a shaking hand holding the gun.

Finally, he spoke without raising his voice. He seemed to be enjoying this game of stealth and terror.

When she looked in the direction of his voice, she saw flames a hundred feet in the air behind him, behind Peralta westerly.

If he was aware, he gave no indication of it. "Listen to me, woman," he said in an almost pleasant voice. "You are mine. I can kill you if I want to. I see you very clearly. . . . Drop the pistol."

When she opened her fingers, the weapon fell.

The renegade told her she was a wise woman. Now she should walk toward the sound of his voice.

Her breath was still coming in gasps when she began walking. There was not a fatalistic bone in Marta's body. If she had to submit to an indignity or die, she would submit, but the man would die if she had to hunt him the rest of her life.

When she was close, the renegade stepped into view, showing white teeth in a wide smile. His voice was still soft as he said, "I think I know who you are. . . . You are returning from starting that fire."

She studied him in silence. He was one of those people whose age is impossible to gauge correctly. He was thick and dirty, with small eyes and pock-scarred cheeks. The little bag tied to his shellbelt rattled when he moved.

"I think I can do better. I can hand you over to *el jefe*. He will trade me money for you. You may be the last to die in this dog of a village. Shot tied to a post as we ride by for starting that fire."

Marta's breathing was almost back to normal, but her heartbeat wasn't. "None of you will leave here," she told the grinning man.

He laughed at her. "You mean because a lot of women are inside the cantina? Listen, *amor*, there is dynamite somewhere, there always is. Someone will tell us where or be blinded. Can your people in the cantina survive two or three sticks of dynamite through the window?"

"Others know you are here. They know Bauman."

He still smiled, but less brightly. "What can they do? It don't matter who knows; they are afraid of us."

Marta took down a deep breath. "No one is afraid of

you—they are only afraid of what you will do. This time you waited too long."

The man finally lost all vestiges of his smile as he gazed steadily at the small woman. She had mentioned the only thing that the marauders feared—staying too long in a raided place—and as had been said at the saloon, that is what they had done at Peralta. They were not night fighters.

The man leaned on the empty house. In Spanish he said, "Listen to me, woman. The others are busy in Gringo-town. Me, I am a businessman. I came down here, and so far without seeing anyone, I have found gold crucifixes, gold rings and necklaces, quite a bit of money in places people like you always think are safe, and which people like me know from experience where to look." The renegade paused, studied Marta for a moment, then continued speaking. "I have three caches. I am ready to quit, go home, buy some nice land with good horses and cattle, a big house. You could come with me. You didn't cry or whine or beg like the others. Listen to me. We can leave this place in the dark. No one will miss me until morning. Those who will miss you"—the renegade shrugged thick shoulders—"in time they will forget about you."

CHAPTER NINE

Blood and Fire

GOD HAD SUBSTITUTED inherent guile for the muscle he had not given women. Marta's stance loosened slightly. Her expression changed. "What is your name?"

The renegade shrugged. "Jose Garcia."

Her reply was given indifferently. "Jose, I don't believe you can get away from here."

He had been challenged. "I could have gotten away from a dozen towns and ranches. In the dark on two good horses . . . What is your name?"

"Marta."

"I know where the best horses are." He paused, gazing at her. "You would go with me for my caches?"

"I was born in this ugly town. I grew up here. When I was younger I dreamed of towns with bright lights instead of candles, people dressed well, dances, even living in a house made of wood with more than one room."

He continued to lounge against the house, looking at her. Eventually he straightened up, ignored a wild gunshot in Gringo-town, and reached for her.

She did not resist; she was warm and soft against him. He leaned back and smiled gloatingly. "Can I trust you, Marta?"

"I told you of my dreams. Can you make them come true?"

He released all but one hand. As he pulled her around,

he said, "More than that. I can promise you better things than you ever imagined."

As they strode past empty *jacals,* he clung to her hand and from time to time turned to look steadily at her.

She smiled, squeezed his fingers when he squeezed her hand. By the time they were north of Mex-town, where he halted to cock his head, then smile and lead off, Marta was close enough so that occasionally they brushed at hip and shoulder.

She gripped his right hand, hard. He looked around, broadly smiling, and returned the hard grip as he said, "I know what you need. Be patient. First we have to—"

The big knife came soundlessly from its sheath and almost as silently plunged halfway to the hilt before the man tried to free his right hand, straightened up to his full height, eyes wide and bulging, and made a gagging sound as he went down.

Marta dropped the knife and ran. This time, with bedlam in Gringo-town, she reached the cantina without difficulty. She beat on the wreckage that barred the doorway and sprang inside before the defenders had completely removed their barricade.

The noise from Gringo-town was mutedly audible. Mud walls three feet thick served several purposes: they kept heat out, prevented rare frost from penetrating, and muffled the loudest sounds.

A large woman whose upper body tapered down to lean thighs and spindly legs threw both arms around Marta. Others crowded close. The men remained at their window and door.

Lupe Villaverde wanted details. They all did, but Lupe was the most persistent questioner. Marta told them of meeting the yardman, of the two strangers on horseback, of lighting the beacon, and of encountering the raider looting Mex-town's residences. When she told them the entire story, only the woman with the barrel chest and spindly legs voiced approval.

The women had seen that brilliant light in the west. Several were of the opinion that the raiders would abandon Peralta as quickly as they could. A few agreed only after suggesting that since the beacon had only recently been lighted, it would take a while for a neighboring town to organize and ride many miles to reach isolated and distant Peralta.

In other words, the marauders would actually not feel compelled to abandon the town immediately.

These women were correct.

In time the excitement that followed the discovery that someone had lighted Peralta's signal of distress died down. In fact, in Gringo-town there was almost none of the racket there had been.

For an excellent reason: Bauman's killers had wrung from their hostages the locations of every known cache, and were now hastily prodding captives toward places known to hold valuables.

This close to acquiring valuable spoils, the raiders intended to pursue their cache hunt before firing the town and fleeing.

From experience they knew that the beacon would be seen and understood, but they also knew from previous scouting that Peralta was miles from even the smallest village.

Their plundering provided time for the women in the cantina to prepare for any incursion from Gringo-town. They were thirsty and there was no water. By starlight the well in the center of the plaza assumed an importance second only to survival.

One of the three men, Miguel, found a large goatskin *bota*. Without knowing whether it leaked or not, he volunteered to attempt filling it from the well.

There were halfhearted words of dissent, for Miguel was

old and withered. Miguel smiled, slung the *bota* from a bony shoulder, and gestured for the other two men to remove the doorway barricade.

The old man turned when Lupe touched his arm and offered a soft prayer for his safety. He nodded to her, ducked through the opening, stopped in front of the building to look and listen, then with surprising speed raced across the open plaza to the well.

Women crowded against the front wall, for once as silent as stones.

The night was less dark than it had been, because the moon had finally arrived. But the moon was thin, and the light from stars was faint. However, it was not poor light that the women held their breath about, it was the groaning sound of the ancient wooden block as Miguel raised a full bucket of water.

It was not a particularly loud noise. The noise from Gringo-town where exultant raiders found riches was louder.

A full bucket of water is heavy. Miguel hoisted two bucketloads before the *bota* was filled to bulging. As the old man strained to hoist the *bota* to the adobe wall encircling the well, which was waist-high, he had to grit his teeth and use every muscle remaining in his old body.

Even then, he only barely got the *bota* on the upper tier of the wall. He paused to suck air and wait for ancient sinews to recover before attempting to get it slung from his shoulder.

Lupe Villaverde made fists of both hands across her middle. Another woman, older than the others, whispered that in her youth she had seen Miguel run across the plaza with such a *bota*. She did not mention that this had been fifty years earlier.

Firelight, which brightened Gringo-town until it was almost as light as day, now reached high enough to cast a whitish glare across Mex-town's plaza.

Miguel grasped the *bota*'s rawhide strap, ran it through his fingers several times, sprung his knees slightly, got the strap across his shoulders, and slowly straightened. He took a staggering few steps. A woman peeking from the barricaded door half-whispered: "He cannot come this far."

Undoubtedly others thought she was right, but no one spoke.

The humpback leaned his carbine aside and began removing the barricade. The other man watching stopped him without saying what was obvious: the man with the crooked back could do no better than the old man was doing.

Every eye was on the water-carrier. They could see the taut sinews in his neck, the glazed look of purpose in his face, the tightly clamped old jaw. Everything about Miguel indicated absolute determination.

He could not walk straight, his legs sagged, he listed first to one side then to the other side. But his face showed only blind resolve; it did not show any of the agony.

Miguel was less than twenty feet from the door when those inside tore aside the barricade, still unsure he would make it but unwilling to have anything in his way.

Concentration was so intense that everything else, including the distant raging fire and the sounds from Gringo-town, were unheeded.

Because of this intentness, when the gunshot sounded no one moved or made a sound for seconds.

Miguel went down; spilling water gushed over him and the dusty ground. One of the men inside groaned and roughly shouldered past the door, stepped outside, and ran to the old man. The *bota* was empty. The old man was floundering and gasping when the other man reached him, hoisted him with surprising strength, flung the old man over his shoulder, and raced back.

He got inside. There was no second gunshot. They placed the old man on the earthen floor. His breathing could be heard throughout the room. Miguel had been stunned by the shot, but he was not wounded.

The older woman who had remembered the water-carrier in their youth, examined the *bota*, ran gnarled fingers over it, and rolled her eyes. In Spanish she said, "The bastard did not try to kill Miguel," and held the *bota* aloft. It had a ragged hole completely through it.

Marta and Lupe exchanged a look. The raiders had not forgotten the forted-up women of Mex-town. The gunman had destroyed their chance to hold out.

Other women who saw the hole either turned away or breathed silent prayers. Some of them had thought that between the beacon fire and the looting going on in Gringotown, Mex-town's defenders would be ignored. Not forgotten, but not attacked either until the renegades had finished plundering and torturing up in Gringo-town. The best they could hope for was a delay, a little time to get ready.

They put the shaken water-carrier beside Poole's bed against the windowless south wall, reinforced the barricade, and waited.

When Miguel had recovered enough to speak, he and Henry Poole talked softly, avoiding what was uppermost in their minds—either a massacre, or rape then a massacre.

Marta and the other women crouched in silence, making sure of ammunition and weapons. Those who had arrived with machetes flung the big knives aside.

The woman who had likened their situation to the Alamo leaned toward Marta and asked why in God's name the possemen had not returned.

Marta had no answer. Neither did anyone else.

The possemen *were* coming. They had started back with two prisoners, hands tied to saddle horns, the survivors of six men who had battled from a jumble of rocks miles northwest of Peralta.

Even after Lee Custis, Juan Morales, Mike Kelly, and the

others saw the fiercely burning beacon, they could not ride any faster. Their animals were used up, head-hung and shrunken.

They could have perhaps raced for town for about a mile. After that, ailing mounts would begin to fall. It was therefore better to slog along, with dread in their hearts but still a-horseback, than to start a panicked run and end up walking.

One of the survivors of the battle in the boulders had been shot through the upper leg as he was trying to mount his horse. The leg had been bandaged, but the man was feverish and very thirsty. When he asked for water, no one replied or even looked at him.

The other prisoner, a brawny, beard-stubbled individual with carroty hair and pale eyes, suddenly laughed.

At the stares he got for this, he explained, "It worked. We ran off some cows, waylaid some riders. Frank said it would work. He said if we got folks in Peralta fired up, they'd make up a big posse and go rustler-hunting."

The redheaded man was defiant even with both wrists lashed to his saddle horn and surrounded by riders who would not hesitate to kill him.

He taunted his captors. "You know what you're goin' to find when you get back?"

Juan Morales rode up beside the prisoner, cocked his gun, and squeezed the trigger. He had shot the gun empty back among the rocks, but he was the only one who knew the gun was empty.

The redheaded man's eyes bulged, his mouth hung open. When Juan's hammer fell on a spent casing, the burly captive looked straight ahead and did not say another word.

His injured companion did, though. He cursed Frank Bauman and several other men whose names meant nothing to his captors.

Clouds appeared from nowhere, unnoticed until a large,

dark one soared across the scimitar moon, causing the land to darken until it passed.

One of the posse riders from Mex-town looked up and crossed himself. Not in his lifetime had there been rain clouds in the Peralta country this time of year.

Tired horses dragged their hind hooves. The trail of the posse riders was marked by those drag marks. Eventually, everyone except the prisoners dismounted and walked beside their animals.

The men looked gaunt and sunken-eyed. They were also beard-stubbled and dirty. Dried salt rings showed at armpits, and shirtfronts were stiff from dried sweat. Some of the posse riders also dragged their feet.

Marshal Custis had said very little since the fight that had resulted in the death of four raiders. He had not mentioned the thought that had occurred to him even before the redheaded prisoner had crowed about Bauman's trick.

He had fleetingly wondered about the marauders' drawing every able-bodied man out of town. The reason he had not dwelt on that hunch was that whoever was out there had deliberately killed three Poole riders and had shot the old man, who was probably dead by now in Mex-town.

He had reacted as any other lawman would have—and any other lawman would have made the same mistake. It was not pleasant to think about, and it would not be as long as he lived, although what he had done had been the normal reaction of most men.

The chill went unnoticed as it increased. Tired men led exhausted horses, trying to ignore the moans of their wounded prisoner.

The moon came and went. Its poor light made the silently trudging men appear as phantasmas, especially since they made almost no noise as they walked beside their horses. Ghostly men with ghostly horses paced down a hushed night with a brilliant beacon of soaring fire miles ahead.

CHAPTER TEN
Fear and Darkness

JAKE REGARDED FRANK Bauman as the last looted cache was being emptied. He was blunt when he said, "We been in this gawddamned village too long, Frank."

Before he could continue, the rawboned man snarled. "I know that. You got any idea how much loot we got? More'n we got at Aromanches. Now we'll fire the wood buildings and ride."

Jake stood in silence for a moment, then was turning away when a man with bloodshot eyes came up and said, "Frank, them bastards killed Jose Garcia." The man, a renegade named Lopez, gestured. "North of town; he's lyin' up there in a pool of blood. I don't know how they done it, but they killed him with that big knife he carried, cut him halfway through." Lopez held up a sack. "This here was lyin' beside him."

The sack was heavy, and wet from Garcia's blood. Jake turned back to say dryly, "He always done that; snuck off to plunder on his own. Sooner or later he was goin' to get caught." The graying man looked at the sack of loot. "The damned fool."

Jake walked away. Bauman and Lopez ignored his departure. Bauman took the sack, looked inside it, and did not hand it back as he said, "Let's get a-horseback."

Lopez hurried away to pass the word of their imminent departure, but Frank Bauman slung the bloody sack over his shoulder and headed for the saloon. He had his share of plunder. Over the years he had developed discrimination: he did not take anything but money. And sometimes he left paper and silver and took only gold coins.

At the saloon he poured a drink, downed it, and looked stonily at his face in the backbar mirror. Even in poor light, the signs of dissipation and ruthless cruelty remained as Bauman's outstanding expression.

He poured a refill and was raising the glass when men began entering the saloon, one or two at a time, most with loot in small satchels or finely woven sacks of the kind Jose had used.

There was little conversation as they lined up along the bar to drink. A thin Mexican downed three shots of whiskey before rearing back and saying, "It had to be a woman. Jose would never let a man get that close." He looked around. "Stuck with his own knife like a goat."

Jake spoke without straightening off the bar or looking around. "We'll remember Peralta. This place took more toll than any other place we rode into."

One man said, "We're wastin' time. We been wastin' it since some son of a bitch snuck out yonder an' lit that fire." The man pushed the glass and bottle violently aside and glared at Frank Bauman. "What are we waitin' for this time, for Chrissake?"

Before Bauman could reply, the sullen-looking Cody spoke his mind. "What about them people forted up in the cantina in Mex-town? Mostly women. I shot the water bag an old man was tryin' to carry from the town well to the cantina. They're thirsty, most likely hungry, and scairt peeless to boot. . . . One of 'em sure as hell killed Jose."

Lopez said scornfully, "Women! Jose ain't the only one they killed." He straightened up with an idea. "Anybody see dynamite when they was lootin' the general store?"

The implication kept everyone silent until Frank Bauman spoke. "There's a stone house out back. I didn't look inside." He looked at Lopez. "Go shoot the lock off. If it's there, bring some back."

As Lopez was departing, Jake finally looked down where Bauman was again raising his whiskey glass. His words fell like steel balls on glass.

"What the hell's the sense of wastin' more time blowin' those women to hell? Frank, they'll be comin' from somewhere. That fire's visible for a hundred miles."

Cody snarled at the older man. "What's the matter, Jake, you didn't find enough loot?"

The older man turned with surprising speed. A fight was imminent. Bauman yelled and swore at them. "We ride after we fling a stick of dynamite into that cantina. Pitch it inside and keep right on riding. No more gawddamned complaining!"

Cody and Jake faced the bar again. Bottles were passed, empties were hurled against the backbar mirror, fresh bottles were opened.

Lopez returned, grinning from ear to ear. He had three cylinders in red waxed paper in one hand. Someone asked about fuse. Lopez fished in a pocket. He had a coil of black cord half as thick as a man's smallest finger.

Jake turned slowly, still irritated and showing it. "All right, now let's get the damned horses and do this, fire the town and ride."

Bauman was the first to walk out into the night. The others followed, several bringing bottles with them.

When they reached the lower end of town, they started catching their horses from the corral where they'd fed and watered them. Only one man commented. "This subbitching town is beginnin' to give me the creeps. Jose didn't kill himself, you know."

No one pursued this topic; they were busy catching horses. Several raiders, having caught their horses, were eyeing Foggy Sommers's animals. They freed their own animals, caught the liveryman's horses, and led them forth to be saddled.

When they were ready to ride, Frank took the dynamite sticks, lashed them together, punched fuse cord down into each one, and handed them to Cody.

"Don't do nothin'," Bauman stated. "We'll go north, come around up there, and ride among them little mud houses. When I stop, the rest of you stop. When I give the word, Cody, you light them fuses, then we'll charge across the plaza shooting. Cody, you swing past that cantina, aim for the window. If you miss, it'll still blow the building to hell. Don't use your gun, just concentrate on gettin' in close and flingin' them lighted sticks. You understand?"

Cody nodded.

Jake objected. "Frank, why take a chance? Around back there's no door or window. Cody could ride down there, dismount, fire the sticks, and place them against the wall."

It was so logical, so simple and safe, that not a word was said among the horsemen, now crowded between two dark, empty *jacals*.

Somewhere near the back of the crowd, a man added, "We could set here. Cody could walk his horse down behind that building—no hurry, no sound, no guns, no danger—take his time placing the dynamite, light the fuses, get astride, and walk his horse on southward. Easy as fallin' off a log."

Frank Bauman sat with both hands resting atop the saddle horn. He could not fault any of this. He knew the others favored it. He leaned, spat, straightened up, and promised himself that first chance he got, he was going to shoot that son-of-a-bitch Jake.

"Cody," he said without taking his eyes off the distant building, "don't make no noise, and take your time." He finally looked at the graying man. "Jake, go with him. If you see so much as a shadow, kill it."

Jake nodded and raised his rein hand as he said, "I'll

make a night-bird call when it's done an' we're ridin' south."

Cody had the dynamite sticks shoved inside his shirt. He had the remaining fuse cord in a hip pocket. He followed Jake. As the others made way, not a word was said.

When the departed riders were out of sight, Grant swung to the ground, leaned on his horse, and said, "Hell of a waste of females, if you ask me."

No one had asked him, and no one answered him. A man among them who was a chronic worrier made a remark that dampened a lot of enthusiasm.

"Suppose someone's out back, maybe among them *jacals* or corrals."

Frank Bauman also swung to the ground beside his horse. He had used blasting powder before. One thing he knew for a damned fact was that one stick of dynamite would rattle doors for a mile. Two sticks, especially placed against a wall, would scatter debris and guts over the countryside.

He was not the only one. Lopez said, "We should move back. Far back. Or maybe ride around where they went so we could all escape together. That cantina is going to be demolished. Not only the cantina."

Bauman was watching the cantina. He showed no evidence of having heard the admonition. Not until he could decently do so did he heed Lopez's advice. He turned casually, not looking at Lopez, rose up across leather, and gestured for those farthest back to turn toward the upper end of Mex-town.

Lopez and a companion exchanged a look. They had expected to be told to pick their way around among the *jacals* until they found a way down behind the cantina.

Now the band would have to flee eastward until they had open country before turning southward to find Cody and the graying man. More wasted time.

Where they halted was near the rain-melted remnant of

the Spanish fort. Several men dismounted. Frank Bauman remained astride. The blast would terrify every horse for a great distance.

A slight chilly breeze blew eastward from the burning beacon-fire. The air smelled of bitter acid; greasewood turned to coals had that kind of smell.

Bauman stirred in the saddle. This was taking too long. A man nearby said, "We all should have gone."

The wait had not actually been that long, but to men with raw nerves made even rawer by whiskey, it seemed an interminable time.

Grant swung off and approached Frank Bauman. "I can ride around over there," he said.

Bauman turned on him with a snarl. "What's the matter with you; they ain't had enough time yet. Shut up an' get back on your horse. When that blast goes off, these animals is goin' to raise hell."

Grant went back and swung astride, his face flushed with anger.

Someone lighted a cigar looted from the general store. The smell was pleasant, and because that vagrant little wind coming from the west had died, the cigar's aroma replaced it.

Bauman swung to the ground, squinted at the position of the moon, and let go a long, loud breath. He should have made them follow his initial idea. If they had, by now they would all be racing miles southward, leaving behind a demolished cantina.

The marauders with bottles sipped, then passed the bottles around, and watched Frank Bauman. Their thoughts were not charitable. Most of them had begun to question his judgment.

Somewhere on the east side of town in roughly the direction of the cantina, a man yelled sharply. His voice was followed by two rapid gunshots. Bauman turned and smiled. "They got some son of a bitch between his *jacal* and the outhouse."

That could have been it. The conditions fit: a startled man between his residence and his outhouse coming upon two raiders in the semidarkness.

If the noise had aroused the people inside the cantina, they would certainly place it as having been somewhere behind the saloon.

Lopez rolled his eyes at his companion.

Bauman turned in his saddle and said, "Get mounted. We'll do this slow and quiet—ride over among them shacks to the east, then turn down behind the cantina."

He led off. Not a word was said, and very little noise was made. There were people, but very few, still in their houses. They listened to the passing horsemen with hearts in their mouths, either clutching crucifixes or trundling rosary beeds through fingers to keep pace with silent prayers.

West of Peralta, the towering flames were diminishing. Within a few hours they would be down to red coals, but the signal had been passed. It had to have been seen in the darkness. That kind of brilliance was visible for hundreds of miles in flat country, even in daylight.

CHAPTER ELEVEN
The Guns of Peralta

BAUMAN AND THE others rode into Mex-town and halted stone-still in front of Cody's body. Nearby was the corpse of a Peralta man Cody had shot. But the shotgun that had killed Cody was a few feet away.

Grant said, "Where's Jake?"

There was no answer as Bauman slowly dismounted and approached Cody's body. "Cody, you damned fool, why didn't you look behind you?"

He moved closer, saw the dynamite sticks lying nearby covered with blood, and rummaged the bloody, ragged pockets until he found the coil of fuse. Bauman retrieved the dynamite sticks. One fuse was lost, but the other one was intact. He cut a length off the coil of fuse and worked at punching the fuse deep into the stick he was gripping.

Bauman went forward to place the dynamite against the cantina wall. He was preparing to kneel when Jake appeared from the south. He was standing in his stirrups, clearly distraught as he gestured frantically.

"Riders down yonder below town. Hell of a mob of them. Frank! You damned fool! Never mind that, get on your horse. We got to go east, and fast. *Frank, gawddamn it . . . !*"

Bauman remained in a bent position, then straightened up holding the sticks of dynamite. But some of the other marauders were already turning easterly. Bauman glared at the graying man. This was not the first time Jake Bentley had taken the initiative. Bauman was motionless, listening to his companions abandoning him.

He dropped the dynamite sticks, walked toward his horse, and when he and Jake were nearly alone, he evened up his reins with his left hand as though to mount. Then he turned, drew, and fired from a distance of less than sixty feet.

Jake flung up both arms as his startled horse tucked up and jumped out from under him.

Several raiders saw the killing. They had hesitated to abandon Bauman up to that moment; now they spun away, racing after their friends.

Inside, the women and men had heard the distraught man's shout. They also heard Bauman's gunshot and the sound of several horses leaving.

Frank Bauman did not charge after the others. He had lost his men, but he had evened the score with Jake for humiliating him.

Even if he caught up with them, he would be treated as a pariah for the killing behind the cantina.

As a hit-and-run marauder, he had been successful. Hitting and running required little more than resolve and a fast horse. He had demonstrated in Peralta that he was incapable of managing a prolonged raid, and that, too, fed the rage in his head.

He mounted quickly, his red fury turned upon the cantina and the people inside it. *Women!* If it weren't for their dogged resistance, this raid would have gone as planned. He knew one way to settle that score.

He dismounted alone behind the cantina and picked up the package of dynamite.

At the edge of town, Marshal Lee Custis led tired men and exhausted horses. They heard a gunshot, and while weariness was too ingrained to be totally ignored, apprehension made them more alert and less concerned with their own condition than at any previous time during their long hike back.

Juan Morales called out, "Something's happened to keep the bastards there. That gunfire sounded like it came from Mex-town."

They left a few possemen to guard the prisoners and take the horses down to the corrals by the livery barn, where they discovered Foggy Sommers's body. Meanwhile, Lee and the rest of the men cautiously headed toward Mex-town.

In the predawn light, they darted down the dark side of the road to the lower end of town, made a wide sashay far below the last buildings walking eastward.

They halted when they heard horsemen riding south-ward from somewhere near the north end of Mex-town. As the possemen were beginning to resume their advance, they heard running horses coming directly toward them. As though by order, but actually by instinct, the possemen sought shelter. Some knelt, some were poised for flight, but none fled, because the riders were approaching too fast.

Marshal Custis saw one rider in advance of the others. He was riding straight up, but there was no mistaking his urgency.

Lee raised his Winchester and waited.

The rider swept to within a couple hundred feet of Lee Custis, who was waiting, thumb pad on the hammer.

Lee let the man come abreast before firing. He was close enough even in poor light to be recognizable as a stranger. He was riding with his left hand full of reins, his right hand balancing a cocked six-gun.

The horse gave a tremendous leap when muzzle blast nearly blinded him on the near side. Its rider bent down, lower, still lower, and finally fell.

Lee waited, then levered up another load, but the sprawling man did not move. The miracle was that his hair-triggered Colt had not fired, either under impact when it struck the ground, or when the man holding it jerked taut when the bullet hit him.

Peralta resounded with gunfire when racing horsemen coming from Mex-town encountered the possemen. The fight was ragged, fierce, and unrelenting until the raiders were beaten back. Without knowing who was trying to kill them, and without a leader to give orders, it became a matter of every man for himself. They scattered in all directions, generally back the way they had come.

The marauders yelled back and forth as they ducked among the adobe hovels, until eventually the gunfire slackened and stopped. The cold oncoming dawn air, utterly still, smelled powerfully of gunsmoke.

Marshal Custis remained in place long enough to reload, then moved stealthily along the back of a house to the corner. There he listened, heard nothing, and bent low before peeking around.

Then there was no movement, no man-shapes in the fish-belly-gray light, not a sound for a long while.

Bauman got back astride and made certain the fuses were in place. He reined his horse southward a dozen yards until he found a wide opening that led to the plaza. He would have to toss the dynamite while riding at a full gallop in order to be safely away before the fuses burned down.

He turned toward the cantina with the dynamite in his lap as he groped in his pockets for a sulfur match.

He lighted the fuses with the cantina dead ahead. He held the dynamite high, gigged the horse into a startled run, and leaned as the distance closed.

At that moment gunfire erupted somewhere in Gringo-town, but it did not sway Bauman as he mounted his final assault on the cantina.

The women and men inside the cantina were not concerned with the gunfire in Gringo-town either. Their attention was on Bauman. They heard him coming. Lupe yelled to the men in the window. One leaned recklessly and saw what the charging rider had in his right hand. Without pulling his head back, he screamed at the women. "Dynamite! He's got sticks of dynamite! Mother of God . . . !"

Lupe and Marta rushed forward. No one else seemed capable of movement—not for moments, anyway. For Marta, aiming through the window opening required standing on her tiptoes. Lupe, taller, shoved her weapon out to find the charging man and aim.

Moving targets are difficult to hit under the best conditions in broad daylight. In darkness, with terror making steady hands impossible, there was the barest chance they could hit Bauman before he got close enough to pitch the burning dynamite either into their building or against it.

Terrified, the women pawed away much of the barricade, settled low, and rested weapons atop the debris. When they heard the man getting closer in a furious run, they leaned, caught sight of him on their left, and resettled their weapons in that direction.

Lupe and Marta fired almost simultaneously. After that the entire front of Morales's saloon was wreathed in foul-smelling gunsmoke. It was impossible to see.

One of the elderly men leaned through the window, beating with his hat to clear the smoke. He might as well have done nothing. The smoke hung without a breath of predawn air to disperse it.

Finally, the distant rattle of gunfire stopped. Marta squirmed through the partially dismantled barricade and swung both arms to clear the smoke away. She was followed by Miguel, who was holding a revolver as long as his forearm. He said, "This way," and went very carefully southward.

She followed.

Very gradually the smoke thinned out. In its place was darkness.

Miguel stopped and pointed. Near where he had fallen when the goatskin bag of water had been shot and emptied was the tall, leggy horse. Ten feet ahead was its rider, facedown in mud, his right hand still locked around the dynamite sticks. When Bauman had been catapulted from his horse, he had slid in the mud another few feet. The dynamite sticks were nearly completely covered with mud. Their fuses had been extinguished when they were dragged through the mud.

Marta and the old man walked over to the fallen man. Within moments they were joined by others. For a while the women and men milled about, saying little. Then a couple of people hurried off to their own homes. Only Lupe and Marta returned to the cantina.

The marshal and the possemen heard the gunfire in Mextown. Lee and a few men moved eastward. When Lee got far enough along to see the plaza, there was a mud hole with a dead man facedown in it. Behind him lay a dead horse.

Juan Morales was more interested in the condition of the nearby building. He said softly, "My cantina." Juan stood up in plain sight. Lee told him to get back, take shelter, but no one shot at him. Apparently, there were no more raiders left in Mex-town.

Juan walked to the front of his saloon, stopped to gaze at its bullet-pocked exterior, at the barricaded opening where a door had been. Heedless of danger, he pushed at the barricade.

Marta had cocked a carbine at him before she saw who he was. Juan did not flinch; he was too tired and too demoralized about what he saw inside. "It is me, Juan Morales," he said as he pushed past the last of the barricade and stepped inside.

Lupe Villaverde was near the bed along the south wall.

She was still holding a six-gun in her hand and had a Winchester within reach.

Juan stood in shock. His cantina was a ruin; the back bar shelves had been swept clean of his inventory. The room reeked of spilled liquor, furniture was broken, and there were abandoned weapons atop his bar.

He turned toward Marta without a word. She spoke quietly. "There was no better place, Juan."

He turned without speaking, went back through the doorway, and said to Lee Custis, "It's ruined. My saloon looks like a whirlwind hit it from the inside. Ruined . . . bottles, tables, chairs, the door . . ."

Lupe came out and quickly summarized what had happened. Lee and most of the others immediately made their way back to Gringo-town, fearful of what devastation they would find there.

CHAPTER TWELVE

"Pronto!"

PERALTA WAS BEGINNING to be drenched with golden light. Except for the stillness and silence, it could have been just another day during the existence of a small town that had been brightened by the same sun for over a hundred years.

When the marshal and his men reached the lower end of Peralta, a tired posseman said, "They got to have horses. They're cut off from gettin' them down here."

Cap Franklin agreed. The former army officer said, "I doubt there's enough private stock corralled around town to mount them all, but that's what they got to do—find horses somewhere."

Juan Morales slipped around back and went stealthily northward until he could see the saloon. He stood in shadows for a long time. When he returned, he told Lee the raiders were all holed up at Kelly's place. Cap Franklin wondered aloud if the possemen could get up there, unseen, and get into hidden places in front of the saloon and behind it.

Mike Kelly listened in stony silence. If the final fight involved his saloon . . . He rolled his eyes in the direction of Juan Morales, whose own establishment had been nearly demolished.

They were turning toward the alley to begin their northward stalk when someone either saw or heard them, and bellowed a warning.

Cap cursed. Mike Kelly moved alongside a building to listen, recognized the complaining sound of his roadway door squeaking open, and went back to tell the others the renegades seemed to be leaving his saloon.

Lee said, "All right; we're going to have to search for them house to house. Now that it's daylight, getting on the east side of town will be dangerous, but it's got to be done. That's where they got to be; they sure as hell won't come to this side."

He was right, but Peralta spread north and south. If the renegades understood what impended, they would not turn their backs and try to reach Mex-town; they would find hiding places on the east side of Gringo-town. They had no alternative, at least until they could find a way to steal some horses and flee.

Leaderless men reverted to the first law of existence: self-preservation and to hell with comrades. The marauders had scattered.

Crossing the deserted, wide roadway in broad daylight was hazardous. Lee took several men with him when he went to the upper end of town and led a dash easterly. No one shot at them—Lee surmised that the desperate renegades were fully occupied with trying to find safe cover.

Cap took some men back in the direction of the livery barn. Down there they emptied every corral and freed the stalled animals. The noise of these animals racing westward from town would be heard by the renegades. For that reason Cap kept his men inside the barn until they could pull a big old wagon inside from Sommers's wagon shed. They went to work putting everything made of wood or leather or metal on the near side against the thick wooden wall, sure that the moment they pushed the wagon into sight they would be fired on from the northern and eastern parts of town.

As the old wagon was trundled forth, given a hard, final push, the men clambered inside. They prayed the momentum would be enough.

It was, but their fear proved accurate too. The wagon was fired on. The rig rolled to a heavy stop when it struck the raised plankwalk south of the general store near the side road going east.

Gunfire was still splintering wood when the possemen scrambled over the front partition, tumbled to the ground, and ran like deer for shelter. By the time the wagon was empty, there were at least eight renegades pouring lead into it.

The possemen huddled around Cap Franklin on the east side of town where the intersecting road led into Mextown. Cap, who was never in a hurry, was in no hurry now. With the wall of a wooden building at their backs, even occasional gunshots posed no particular threat. When he was satisfied all were accounted for and uninjured, he told them they now had to work their way north, watching both sides of the alley separating the two parts of Peralta.

He led them to the corner of their protective building, peeked around, saw nothing, and gestured for them to start their stalk.

At the same time, someone at the opposite end of town howled a curse and fired a rifle. Not a carbine or a handgun, but a long-barreled rifle. The men with Lee Custis sought cover and waited. To Lee, the gunshot had seemed to come from midtown and overhead. He removed his hat, got belly-down, and eased his head around. In daylight, telltale puffs of burnt gunpowder were difficult to find. The longer a man looked, the more invisible they became.

He wiggled backward, got to his feet, and was putting his hat on when Abe Thompson shook his head and sprayed tobacco juice. "Atop the store," he guessed. "Maybe if I go down the alley I can get down there."

Mike Kelly growled. "You even look into that alley an' you'll eat supper in hell."

Surprisingly, a gunshot sounded on the west side somewhere in the vicinity north of Sommers's barn. Moments later, a bridled horse with no saddle raced southward down the alley and out of town. A dying raider was sitting on the ground beside the shed where he had found the saddle animal, his gaze fixed steadily on the window hole where the shot had come from.

Framed in the window, poised to fire again, was the nursing mother who had been terrorized by Bauman and his men.

She and the man she had shot looked at each other for a long time. The wounded man had a holstered Colt near his right hand.

The woman slowly re-aimed her weapon over the sill and cocked it. The man beside the animal shed slowly shook his head.

She remained motionless, gunstock snugged back, until he very slowly went sideways in the dust. She did not relax her position for a long time, not until she was satisfied her shot had done what she had intended it to do.

Lee's men were unable to advance southward in the alley. Every time there was a noise or movement back there, hidden snipers fired.

The sun was climbing; it was still chilly, though, which heightened perception of distances. Mountains that were ordinarily smoke-hazed stood out clearly. Everything in Peralta, every dead man in the roadway, every smashed window and door, every barricaded place, stood in sharp detail.

Several of Cap Franklin's men managed to elude detection and approach the middle of town from the alley. They, like their enemies, had no visible targets, but since they knew their town, suspected where they might flush out a renegade, they occasionally fired into those places.

They were not always challenged by return fire. Cap was behind a huge oak barrel when he yelled for the marauders to pitch out their weapons because there was not a chance in hell they were going to see sunset. That got a response: a veritable fusillade of shots raked the alley, several even striking Cap's barrel. He did not do that again.

Among the leaderless raiders, two men inside Kelly's saloon flung bottles into the roadway, where they shattered, drenching the dust with liquor. For a while this made no sense—not until the roadway was literally paved with broken glass. The hurlers moved to the back of the saloon to repeat their destruction in the alleyway.

Lee realized the reason for the glass was to make it impossible for anyone to rush the building in front or back.

Sniping was intermittent, but threatening and persistent. Not until the sun was nearing its zenith did there appear to be a slackening in the gunfire from among the renegades.

Men from both ends of town stopped firing but continued to seek places closer to the saloon, until a venomous-sounding voice yelled from somewhere in the vicinity of the saloon.

"Watch out front, you bastards!"

A woman staggered out of the saloon and braced herself against a wall, seemingly on the verge of collapse. There was not a sound. She seemed to breathe deeply before stumbling across the road in the direction of the harness shop.

Beside Mike Kelly, Abe Thompson stood, erect and white. The woman was his wife. He began to rush out. Mike Kelly caught him from behind, held him with a powerful grip despite the short man's writhing.

Mrs. Thompson reached the shop across the road, turned, and listlessly sank to the ground. Abe ran to her aid. From the saloon an unseen man laughed. After that he called loudly, "You see her, you sons of bitches? Well, we got three more in here. . . . If you want 'em alive, you better round up a lot of horses and tie them out front."

The silence following this call was not broken until the same taunting voice called again. "You hear me? Better commence leadin' them up here; next one won't be able to walk out. We'll cut her damned throat and roll her out!"

Kelly growled to no one in particular, "They'll do it. Don't none of you ever doubt it."

Somewhere farther south, Cap Franklin pressed in a recessed doorway, anxiously watching. The men who had heard that promise would be murderously angry, and that was when men got reckless.

He called an admonition without much hope. "Steady. We'll get 'em. Steady!"

Abe shielded his wife as they made their way toward their house. Only a few men noticed; both raiders and possemen were concerned with more immediate problems.

Lee settled his back against a building. Around him, men were motionless. It was no longer a battle; it had now become something different, and none of them seemed willing to define it.

Juan Morales's Mex-town companions conversed softly, with Juan shaking his head at each suggestion. One man walked away. No one stopped him; since he was heading for Mex-town they assumed he was going home, and that was all right. They needed every gun, but not everyone could go through all they had gone through for the past couple of days.

With silence came an awareness of rising heat. The sun was off center, the sky was cloudless, and in the distance there was a noticeable heat haze.

Mike Kelly had systematically reloaded his gun before relighting a limp cigar. An older man hunkered, leaning on his carbine and gazing northward where mountains appeared as smoky scraps of bent cardboard.

Lee straightened up. "We couldn't give them horses even if we wanted to. We turned 'em all loose."

Kelly growled. "We got us a standoff."

Marta Sandoval joined them from the east, still carrying a handgun because she had no belt or holster for it. She had heard what was going on, she told Marshal Custis. She held out something soggy and mud-covered. It was the sticks of dynamite whose fuses had been extinguished when Frank Bauman fell in the mud out front of Juan's cantina.

Lee looked, sighed, and said, "Thanks, but this stuff won't detonate, Marta. It's soaked clean through."

She smiled at him. "I know, but *they* don't know."

The men gazed steadily at her. She held out the dynamite for Lee to take as she said, "I don't have any fuse. If you can make a fuse and light it, someone could sneak along the wall and pitch it into the saloon. They don't know it won't explode, so they'll have to come out."

Lee held the limp sticks. He raised his eyes slowly. Kelly looked hopeful for the first time in about half an hour. He took the dynamite from Lee, dug out a huge blue bandanna, and wiped each stick free of mud. He squinted as he held them up. Their waxed-paper exterior, designed to protect the dynamite sticks from being dampened, looked to be in excellent condition. Water had run in from the top, where forcing fuses in had broken the sealant.

Custis took back the dynamite and studied each stick. Without looking up, he said, "What do we use for a fuse?"

Kelly pulled his shirttail out. "Cut it, twist it hard."

Lee used his pocketknife to cut some shirting, examined each strip carefully, then began twisting the cloth. When he had done that, he said, "Kerosene."

Kelly took the rags and ducked into a nearby building. He soaked the rags in kerosene from the first lamp he found.

When he got back to the others, he used the marshal's

knife to gouge at the top of each dynamite stick until he had adequate openings, then worked the rags down with the point of his knife.

When he finished, he was smiling. He held the sticks of dynamite out to Lee.

Marta reached for the dynamite. Kelly had a gathering frown as he said, "Are you crazy? Let me have that stuff."

She twisted from his reach. "We have some men in the alley. Find them, tell them to fire into the back of your building. When the renegades fire back, I will run past and fling the dynamite inside."

Kelly said, "You *are* crazy." He would have taken the dynamite from her, but she was quicker. She went to the corner and leaned to look out as she told them to get the men in the alley to fire into the back of the saloon.

Her final words were: "Keep it up, lots of guns." She looked over her shoulder. "Well, what are you waiting for? *Rapido! Pronto!*"

CHAPTER THIRTEEN

Marta's Idea

MARTA'S TEENAGED NEPHEW called softly to her, eased up beside her, and persuaded her to hand him the dynamite. He shouldered her out of the way and leaned to look southward. There was no one in sight; the entire length of the roadway was silent and still. She told him to wait, which he did. She ran back to wait with the marshal.

When gunfire erupted out back, lots of it and deafeningly loud, the young Mexican lighted each kerosene-soaked "fuse," took down a deep breath, flattened against the nearest roadway building, and without haste but with extreme caution, moved southward toward the spindle doors of Kelly's saloon.

Lee looked at Marta, who did not appear shaken by the crescendo of gunfire. He could not say anything because of the racket in the alley, but he marveled at her ingenuity and toughness. She epitomized courageous quick-thinking.

The embattled marauders were firing into the alley from every place they could use a weapon. They had puffs of oily smoke to aim at, but no human targets. A grizzled raider screamed above the gunfire. "They're softenin' us up, then they'll rush the door."

It was a reasonable idea, even though it was completely incorrect.

Lee reached for Marta's hand and gripped it hard when

her nephew held the smoking fuses away from his body, paused to make a final gauge of the distance, then ran like a deer until he was in front of the spindle doors, where he halted, aimed high, and threw the dynamite sticks. They sailed over the top of the twin doors. Marta's nephew fled southward, aiming for a dogtrot. He did not make it. Someone fired at him from across the road. When he fell, his aunt held both hands to her mouth. Seeing the puff of gunsmoke, Lee aimed carefully and fired. Someone inside a building on the west side of the roadway squawked in pain.

Marta's nephew got up onto all fours, hung there bleeding before forcing himself upright. Now when he ran he dragged his right leg.

The noise was deafening; gunfire from the alley continued, and restless possemen at both the middle and upper end of town were cursing and yelling.

Marta's nephew dragged himself down through the dogtrot and collapsed back there. A posseman using the same opening between two buildings looked around and saw the lad. He turned his back on the alley and knelt to rip the youth's trousers, consider the bleeding injury, then tore cloth from his shirt to fashion a tourniquet, using his gun barrel to twist until the bleeding stopped.

Behind the dogtrot, yelling men at the saloon paused in their firing to look back where the fuses were giving off pungent dark smoke. For several seconds they stared as if incapable of believing what they saw. Then, with wild shouts they raced toward the spindle doors, bursting outside and firing wildly as they scattered. One man and three women remained in Kelly's saloon. The women were tied and the man had been shot through the body. He stared unwaveringly at the burning fuses.

In hot sunlight, possemen were waiting at the upper end of town. When the panicked raiders burst out of the saloon firing wildly and yelling, it was an intimidating sight. Although the men with Marshal Custis peeked around the corner of their protective building and were actually in no great danger since the panicked outlaws were firing out of fear, neither looking for targets nor seeing any, several possemen shot back and missed by wide margins.

Lee pushed Marta out of harm's way. She returned and fired her six-gun empty.

For moments the rattled raiders yelled as they fired and fled among the buildings opposite Kelly's place. In that brief span of time only one raider was brought down. He lay half on, half off the west-side plankwalk.

Cap's bull-bass voice rose above the racket as he yelled for the men in the alley to find ways through toward the main roadway.

Some made it, most did not, but by the time they did the raiders were out of sight among buildings on the west side of town.

For moments there was another interlude of quiet.

Men who had scarcely moved were panting as though they had been running. Marta turned away and hurried eastward. Those who saw her depart said nothing; they knew where she was going and hoped very hard that what she would find would not cause tears.

While Juan and Lee were talking, an old man named Asa Flowers announced that it might have been better if the dynamite had blown the saloon up, because now all they had accomplished was to scatter the outlaws on the west side of town where they would probably have to be hunted down one by one.

Part of his reasoning was sound, but the part about blowing up Kelly's saloon was met with silence—there were hostages in there.

Cap Franklin appeared among the marshal's possemen, dirty, disheveled, and sweat-soaked. He was brusque. "Now someone can shoot the alley door open and get the women out of the saloon."

Juan Morales jerked his head. Four men went with him, and although there was reason to believe no renegades were still on the east side of Peralta, they were very cautious, particularly when they stood exposed as Morales shot the alley door open.

Kelly's saloon was devastated. The damage was greater than that at Juan's cantina, because Kelly's saloon was larger, more extensively stocked, and had more furnishings.

They untied the women, who then left through the alley. One of them, a dumpy, hard-eyed Mexican, guided the other two women to Mex-town, which was mostly quiet now and seemed deserted. She handed them over to Lupe Villaverde to tend.

The renegade lying in blood inside the saloon was dead. Juan made certain of this before he and his men went back up where the other possemen waited.

Cap Franklin told everyone bluntly what they now had to do, and Cap did not minimize the peril; he had been on skirmishing manhunts before. "You are the hunters, they are the hunted. That means you got to push the fight, take all the risks. They'll be hiding, most likely in houses, and they'll have eyes in the backs of their heads." He paused, seemed about to say more, changed his mind, and said gruffly, "Good luck."

Lee welcomed Cap's expertise. He stood still and silent, knowing that what Cap did not say is they had been lucky so far; they'd had shelter and their enemies had been forted up. But from here on, they would almost certainly take casualties.

Asa Flowers leaned on his Winchester, impassive and thoughtful. He had never been a soldier as had Cap Franklin, but he'd been in his share of Indian fights, and in his view this was going to be about the same: ducking, dodging, using stealth, being as wary as wolves and probably getting shot in the back.

He jettisoned his cud, cleared his throat, and shook his head. Kelly asked if he was worried. The old man answered honestly, "Yep, plenty worried. Only way I know for us not to get massacred is to fire the wooden buildings an' force the bastards out where we can see them."

For the second time, his judgment was considered in total silence.

Lee and Juan Morales exchanged a look. The cantina owner said, "That's exactly what this damned fight is all about—saving the town."

Old Asa put a jaundiced gaze on Morales. "Ain't nothin' in your part of town that'll burn."

Stung, Juan turned on the old man. "This is past being about your part of town or my part of town. We have to kill those sons of bitches, but not by doin' what they would do—burning Peralta."

The old man fished for what was left of his cut plug, leaned his Winchester aside, and meticulously picked off lint. He'd given his opinion; now it was up to the others.

Cap gestured with a massive arm. "They're over yonder; they've had time to fort up any place they can while we been talking. They're watching over here sure as Gawd made green apples. We have to take the fight to them, which means cross the road. Unless someone can come up with something better."

No one could. They now understood what Cap had been silent about: the worst, most deadly part of their battle was yet to come.

The sun was tainted with dust as it began its long slide toward the mountain-marked westerly horizon. It was red.

One of the men from Mex-town thought they should take turns getting something to eat, and when dusk arrived to meet again and cross the roadway when it would be difficult for the outlaws to see them.

It was a reasonable idea, particularly the part about getting something to eat, but even Juan Morales did not speak out in favor. He had another idea, one that caught Cap Franklin's attention.

"Some of us stay up here, make a little noise now and then, maybe even call to them. The rest of us go down the alley to the lower end of town, walk a mile or so southward until they can't possibly see us, then turn west and sneak up the alley behind them."

For a moment no one spoke. When they did, Lee asked Cap if he thought the idea was sound. Cap did and turned to lead the way, leaving it up to the others to decide who would leave and who would stay.

Asa was one of the five men who stayed.

Cap walked fast; it troubled him that dusk might arrive before they could finish this affair. He had no desire to hunt desperate men in the dark, and he had even less desire for this fight to linger until tomorrow. None of them had eaten lately. A dull mind made men careless, and that would be fatal.

Incredibly, fragrant supper-fire smoke reached them from Mex-town as they passed southward hidden from sight of the men across the road, testimony to the fact that life goes on under even the most trying circumstances.

There was almost no conversation as the possemen proceeded. When they reached the hushed, gloomy lower end of town, Cap's stride did not slacken. He was marching them like soldiers. When they were several hundred yards southward, someone yelled from the upper end of town. This shout was followed by two very rapid gunshots.

Lee wondered if someone among the renegades was not a very accomplished *pistolero*. Very few men could fire a single-action .45 so rapidly that the blast of the second shot rode over the noise of the first shot.

Cap halted. The afternoon sun was casting shadows, providing the first cooling since dawn or shortly after.

He squinted northward until he was satisfied it was safe, then jerked his head and briskly hiked west until they could all see Sommers's barn, which was the last structure, except for shacks, at the southern end of Peralta.

He then jerked his head to lead them northward in the direction of the west-side alley. Lee squinted at the sinking sun. He did not at all like the idea of returning to town while there still was enough daylight for them to be seen, even though they might not be expected.

CHAPTER FOURTEEN
Mexican Standoff

DAYLIGHT HAD A coppery cast and dusk was still in the offing. Cap stood in the gloomy barn runway telling them all he knew to help them stay alive and still press the fight, which was neither very much nor very reassuring.

Lee and Juan stood together in the alley opening. The town was quiet except for an occasional gunshot. Morales shook his head. "They must have taken a lot of ammunition from the store."

Lee nodded, although his concern was not bullets, but rather the houses with killers inside them using hostages. Cap Franklin came back to also look up the alley. He did not say a word; he gestured for the others to come to the alley and pointed. Three men darted across into a network of old corrals and disappeared. Cap made a rattling sigh as he continued to study the alley. Lee said, "They'll have human shields."

Cap nodded, still looking, still silent.

There was a brisk exchange between the forted-up raiders and townsmen at the upper end of town. When the echoes were dying, a man shouted from somewhere on the west side of town.

"Listen, you bastards. We got hostages. Women and children. We don't aim to harm 'em, but that'll be up to you. We'll trade you a woman or a kid for a horse. One on one."

Someone at the north end of town yelled back. "There ain't no horses. We emptied the livery barn an' the corrals."

Cap nudged Lee and gestured. While this exchange was in progress, Cap led them across the alley among residences. They placed the house the raider was calling from; it belonged to the proprietor of the general store. It was large, well-maintained, and had a number of genuine glass windows.

There was a high picket fence out back. The gate was in the middle where a large shade tree grew. Inside the yard someone—certainly not the storekeeper, who had no time for such things—had a well-tended and rather extensive flower garden, an uncommon sight in Peralta.

"You find horses," the outlaw called. "They ain't all gone. You find 'em, saddle 'em, and lead 'em out where we can see 'em."

"And," came the shouted reply, "you'll set the women an' kids free where we can see 'em?"

The outlaw laughed. It sounded like a steel rasp going over tin. "You get the damned horses, out where we can see 'em."

The yelling ceased as Cap gestured his companions to scatter. Juan Morales passed down the side of a house until he could see the back of the storekeeper's residence. On the opposite side of the same house the marshal got into place.

It was a tantalizing sight, that big house where it seemed some—maybe all—the renegades had forted up, but neither Lee nor Juan Morales considered trying to cross the alley to throw themselves down where the flowers were tallest.

Lee was backing away from the corner of the house when a thin-sounding male voice said, "I seen four of 'em go in over there."

Lee looked up at the white face framed in a window. He knew the man, knew his wife and youngsters. He nodded and returned his attention in three directions. For safety's sake, he assumed not all the renegades were over there.

The man at the window raised his voice to a stronger whisper. "I think there's one in Clanahan's cow shed yonder." Clanahan's shed was south of Marshal Custis. It had a faggot corral around most of it. The distance over there was not great, but it was totally without cover.

Lee returned to the southwest corner of the house, utilized an adjoining residence to move to his right, paused to look out back, and got flat down to peek around. He was lying like that, listening for sounds and watching for movement, when Cap spoke behind him.

"Marshal, it'll be dark directly. They'll slip away in the dark. We don't have enough time to smoke them out. If we get in a hurry, folks are going to get killed."

Lee held up his hand for silence. He thought he had seen movement through the slats of the faggot corral.

He saw it again, low and moving eastward. What kept him from firing was the color and the height, which was just as well—otherwise, he might have killed someone's milk goat.

He pushed back around to the rear of the house and stood up, beating dust off. Cap spoke again. "It comes down to—do we want them bad enough to maybe get folks killed, or do we want them to get away from Peralta? It'll be dark directly. Fighting house to house in the dark—believe me, I know—don't work."

Juan Morales came along with two companions. Cap looked at them in silence. It was the marshal's decision.

Lee leaned on the house. "You mean palaver, Cap?"

The large older man made a slight shrug and said nothing.

A solitary gunshot sounded. It could have come from among the houses or it could have come from the upper end of town. Wherever it came from, there was no second shot.

Lee finally spoke. "They want horses, Cap. Nothin' we can say is goin' to make any difference unless we agree to give them horses, and that depends on how many we can find an' how many raiders there are."

Cap nodded almost stoically. "That's what I'm talking about. Palaver."

Morales grunted. "An' it'll get dark."

Cap nodded. "It's going to do that anyway. We can't smoke them out before dark."

For a long time no one spoke. There were no more gunshots. Unexpectedly, the same harsh-voiced man called into the silence.

"You gettin' them horses? If you don't do it quick, we're goin' to commence crackin' skulls. You understand me?"

Lee knew the others were watching him. He lifted his hat, scratched, dropped the hat back in place, and nodded.

He answered the forted-up renegade, but from westerly, across the alley behind the house where the outlaw had called from. "How many horses do you need?"

There was no reply for a long time. Evidently the men in the storekeeper's house had not expected an answer from out back. There was no sign of them at the back of the house, but that did not mean at least one or two of them had not gone back there.

The harsh-voiced man replied to Lee Custis, "You just get them out front, rigged to ride, where we can see them."

A Mexican standing with Juan Morales spoke softly. "He don't know about the others. He don't know how many of his friends are left."

The others considered that, decided it was probably correct.

Lee called for the last time. "All right, but we got to search in Mex-town, too. It'll take time."

The renegade answered curtly, "Get to doin' it. Don't drag your feet. If we don't see horses directly, we're goin' to start bustin' heads and roll the bodies out to you."

The soft-spoken Mexican made another deduction. "He didn't say shoot, he said crush heads. I'll guess they're low on ammunition."

That could be correct also, but no one wanted to test it. Morales told Lee he'd go see what could be found in Mex-town, although he knew that while there were burros and a small mule here and there among the corrals, there were very few horses.

He turned away in the late-day shadows with dusk close at hand.

Lee looked around as other townsmen, who had heard the shouting back and forth, appeared soundlessly. Fortunately the light was poor; otherwise the marshal would have seen his own reflection in the haggard, stubbled, soiled men around him.

Cap had an idea. "You go north and I'll go south. If we find anything they can ride, we'll meet in an hour or so."

The men split up and departed, unwashed, tucked-up scarecrows. People in dark houses saw them pass. There was not a sound, not even barking dogs.

Peralta was steeped in an eerie quiet. There were no lights, except here and there in Mex-town where people covered windows with blankets. If these were sufficiently moth-eaten, tiny pinpricks of candle glow showed through.

Lee had three men with him. One man knew where there was a combination horse, one trained to accept a rider as well as a harness. They went after it. The animal was slick and docile. It allowed itself to be rigged out and led forth.

They also found a tall Missouri mule that met them at the gate of its corral with big ears forward and intelligent tawny eyes showing either suspicion or curiosity. Mules being what they are, it was probably more the latter than the former.

The mule was muscled-up and fairly young. One man went into the corral and returned shaking his head. He'd found a driving harness but no saddle. The question was whether the mule could be ridden.

Lee went over, leaned hard on its back. The big mule cranked its measly tail, flattened both big ears, and turned to bite.

They closed the gate after themselves and continued their search.

They got a surprise at the lower end of the alley. Four horses were standing against the corral stringers across the alley.

It required a little "chumming" to catch all four. Afterward they led the animals inside, watered them, and rigged each for riding.

Lee said, "Five. That's better'n I expected."

They retraced their route until they were north of the storekeeper's dark, forbidding residence, then fanned out again to complete a northward sweep.

The searchers knew their town, every corral, every shed and barn in it. As they progressed northward they found almost no animals, although there was evidence that animals had been corralled. Apparently, others had turned their horses loose to avoid having them stolen by the raiders.

Behind the stage company's yard there was a high adobe wall with a wide gate in the middle. It was barred from the inside by a massive *tranca* secured by four steel hangers.

The gap between both sections of the gate was sufficiently wide to accommodate a long knife-blade but not wide enough for anything thicker.

A posseman shoved his boot knife through, got it below the *tranca*, but because the bar was heavy and because he could not get enough leverage with a knife handle, he could not raise the bar.

The wall was eight feet tall and smooth. There was one way to open the gate from the alley, which was to find something thin enough to go through the gap and long enough for several men to lean on it to raise the *tranca*.

Cap swore under his breath. They had already used up more than an hour. He backed against the wall, made a stirrup of both his ham-sized hands, and nodded in the direction of a tall, thin man. When the man stepped into his hands Cap sprang his knees upward, shot the man high enough to sidle over the top, clamber down the other side, and lift the *tranca*.

Inside, there was a disappointment. There were at least a dozen sets of heavy harness on hooks in the storage room, but no saddles.

There should have been at least ten animals in the corrals; there were four, and one had a bad limp. Lee entered the corral to examine the other three. They seemed sound enough, and were fairly tractable. He led them out, handed shanks to different men, closed the gate on the limping animal, and looked skeptically at their latest acquisitions.

Stage companies used harness horses. Harness horses, as a rule, were not riding horses unless of course they were combination horses. But the horses Cap, Lee, and the others were looking at had no white chafe marks on the withers, a sure sign of old saddle sores, although they had white hair from old collar sores.

They took the horses out into the alley and turned northward. They were close to the upper end of town. Lee walked on the left side of a big horse he was leading, the others followed his example, and the entire cavalcade crossed the wide main thoroughfare without haste. If the desperate raiders saw them, they also saw their foemen were protected by the horses, their only hope of salvation.

There was no sign of the men who had been on the east side of Peralta at the upper end, but as they looked for something to tie their animals to, Cap cocked his head. A horse whinnied loudly near the opposite end of town. Cap shook his head with vehemence. "Stud horse; what did they fetch him along for?"

A quiet voice came out of the dusk to them. It was not a man's voice. "It only matters that we may have enough horses."

Marta came out of the gloom. She finally had someone's shellbelt around her middle to support the six-gun she'd previously had to carry in her hand.

Lee asked where the other possemen were. Marta gestured. "South of Kelly's place by now." She lowered her arm and examined the horses. "No more?" she asked.

One of the men with Lee was annoyed. "Lady," he told her, "we're lucky we found these. How many the others got?"

"Six from Mex-town," she replied. "Three mules and three horses." She looked at the haggard men. "They won't be back up here for a while. Come with me and get fed."

Cap said he would remain with the horses, they could bring food back to him. Lee also remained with the horses. The others, with Juan Morales and Marta up ahead, went briskly toward Mex-town. Juan told her of the proposed trade. She already knew; that renegade with the harsh voice could be heard a considerable distance, particularly on a quiet night.

Lee sank down. Cap went back to the corner of the building, returned after a while, and said, "There's a light in your jailhouse."

Lee was not surprised. It had occurred to him, when the raiders were stampeded out of Kelly's saloon and got among the buildings on the same side of town as the *juzgado*, that sooner or later some of them would break into the jail, shoot locks off the doors.

He thought briefly of the confident, defiant prisoner. If someone put a gun into his hand, he would be a deadly enemy of the possemen who had killed four of his companions, had seriously wounded another one, and had threatened to kill him.

Cap sank down with his back to a building. He was dog-tired, hungry, and not convinced things were going to turn out as he, and others, wanted them to.

He was a pipe smoker but had neither his pipe nor tobacco, and that added to his gloom. He watched the lawman going among the tied animals to make a better inspection than they'd had time for earlier, and said, "Their kind don't make a clean swap." Cap sighed. "It's different with soldiers; they do all this for principle, because they believe they're defending something. When soldiers trade prisoners, they keep their word. These worthless sons of bitches have no principles, don't care about anything except killing and looting. You can't put trust in anything they tell you.

"My guess is that they'll take some of the women with them, use them for shields. Maybe they'll set them loose after they're away from town, and more'n likely they won't."

Lee came over and also sat down. "We got to wait and see," he said. "At least we got contact, the gunning's stopped."

Cap gazed into the dark distance, silent for a time. Eventually he spoke again. "I guess we can hope. There's nothing else. How many do you reckon are still alive?"

Lee had no idea. He was not even sure how many had attacked Peralta. Someone had said that originally there had been over twenty raiders.

When he did not reply, Cap made a guess. "I think we've shot up about six or eight of them, but that's only a guess. . . . And if Marta's right, we got altogether about a dozen saddle animals, of which some, like the critters we got from the corral yard, may not be broke to saddle. . . . Likely not enough, unless the fellers scouting behind town can come up with another few head.

"Anyway, I got a bad feeling. Those men are plain killers; dogs, horses, women, kids, or us."

Lee was tired to the bone, and thirsty. He rocked against the wood at his back and closed his eyes. Cap nudged him; he had heard the others returning from Mex-town.

He and Lee were on their feet when Marta appeared with the others, bringing food. Lee eyed the small woman, marveling at her appearance; she neither looked nor acted tired, and yet she had been through as much as the men. When she handed him an *entomotado* wrapped in corn husk, she smiled.

He accepted the food and smiled back. "Quiet down yonder, eh?"

She nodded, smile fading. "They are laying out the dead. They've had plenty of practice."

He asked her how many renegades they had down there. She answered without hesitation. "Five."

Lee ate and made another rough estimate. He came up with more than he had thought earlier, which was unsettling.

Marta said they had nine wounded in Mex-town, not including her nephew, who had been shot through the fleshy upper part of his leg and was now being cared for. She put her head slightly to one side as she gazed at Marshal Custis. "Lupe Villaverde has many talents: nurse, doctor, cook, fighter."

He remembered something and looked down. "I guess old Henry Poole was too far gone for her to save him."

Her dark eyes widened. "He did not die. We took him into the cantina with us and—"

"But I was told there was a burial about the time the raiders came."

Marta's expression changed. "That was Lupe's grandfather. He died in his sleep. We all went to the burial with her."

Cap came over from talking with the other men. He had

finished his food and was now more thirsty than ever. He told Lee and Marta he was going for some water and left them.

He failed to get his drink; quiet men came up the alley, leading animals. Cap saw and recognized them before he got anywhere near an *olla*. He moved into the middle of the alley to ask how many animals they had found.

The answer was five head.

Cap said nothing as he turned back to walk with the others to the north end of town where Lee and his companions were waiting.

By Cap Franklin's estimate, they did not have enough saddle animals.

CHAPTER FIFTEEN

Deadly Darkness

THERE WAS TALK about what the renegades would do to their hostages when they knew there would not be enough saddle horses for all of them to escape on.

The townsmen had no way of knowing that some of the raiders had already fled, in darkness and on foot, convinced no one would survive the battle in Peralta.

As for the shortage of saddles, the harness maker's shop always had five or six racked-up saddles for sale.

However, despite darkness, if they led animals down there to be rigged out, the raiders would hear them. To forestall blind shooting in darkness, Cap suggested that someone engage the raiders in a palaver while others took the animals down there to be saddled.

"Don't tell them how many critters we got," Cap said to Lee Custis. "Just that we're trying to get enough outfits."

The marshal accepted what the others evidently seemed to have agreed upon without a discussion: Lee would palaver.

Some prescient soul handed around a goatskin *bota* of water. Cap Franklin finally got to quench his thirst. Others did the same. Lee was the last, and the *bota* was light by the time he took it.

He put down the depleted bag, turned, went to the edge

of the building where he could see the full length of Peralta's main thoroughfare, and called.

A human voice in the dark hush hanging over Peralta carried well, but the response was not immediate, and when it eventually came it was not in the voice of the harsh-toned man. The answering renegade had a noticeable Mexican accent. He said, "You damned near run out of time. Where is the horses?"

Without mentioning that all the animals were not horses, nor their total number, Lee explained about the lack of saddlery and what was being done about it.

The accented renegade replied roughly. "Lead them out where we can see them."

Lee's reply was equally brusque. "Sure. As soon as you turn a hostage loose so we can see him, or her."

Moments later, a door was yanked open and almost immediately slammed closed.

Up the road on the same side of the roadway as the *juzgado* and the storekeeper's house, listening possemen nearing the front of the saddle and harness shop reacted to the demand to see animals by leading several to the center of the roadway.

At the same time, a frightened child of about nine or ten crossed the road like a sleepwalker. Lee reached, pulled him close by the shoulder, and waited for the renegades to see the horses.

A different voice called out after the animals had been seen. It was no less venomous but sounded slightly more reasonable when its owner said, "All right. Now listen close. When they're rigged out, lead 'em all down here, you hear me? Each feller leadin' a horse stays with the animals. No guns, no knives, not one bad move, or we'll shoot every one of them. An' the rest of you—not one shot or we'll put this house to the torch with the folks inside tied to chairs. . . . You, over there, what's your name?"

"Lee Custis. What's yours?"

There was no answer for a while, until another voice, slightly higher than the other two, called back. "Marshal Custis! All right, lawman, we know who you are. Now, you get them horses rigged and down here real quick, or the killing begins. *Pronto.*"

Lee had a question. "How many are you?"

"Just lead the gawddamned animals down here! You hear me, or do you want us to kick out a woman with two busted arms?"

Lee's voice did not change when he called again. "Reason I asked is because we dug up every critter we could find. We got about fourteen animals. There isn't another one anywhere close, unless you'll take burros."

The reply was quick and surprising. "Fourteen's enough. Get 'em rigged out and led down here. . . ." For a long moment, when Lee thought their conversation had ended, the renegade was silent. Then he yelled again, in a lighter tone of voice. "Hey, lawman, we come up with somethin' better—have your women lead them critters down here. You won't shoot your women when we come out."

Lee did not answer, but northward a short distance a man swore loudly. His reply from the renegades was loud laughter.

Lee watched the men and animals across the road northward, where bridles and saddles were being brought out of the harness works and cinched onto warm backs. He saw Marta among those men; she was telling them something. When they finished saddling and bridling, they remained in front of the leather works instead of leading animals out where the renegades could see them.

Lee fidgeted. The forted-up renegades had probably raided every closet and cupboard in the storekeeper's house, which should, if any residence in Peralta should, have been well provisioned. They had water, too.

He alternately watched the men up in front of the saddle

and harness shop, and the front of the house across the road. He was startled when someone called from over there.

"Where's them damned animals? Mister lawman, you remember—one bad move an' we'll pile dead women an' kids up in here until hell won't hold 'em all!"

Cap heard that snarling shout, jerked his head, and led the procession of animals. At once two mules and one harness horse busted loose. None had ever had a saddle on their backs before.

The men leading other horses got animals on each side of the fighting livestock and squeezed, and pummeled, them into at least temporary docility.

They reached the center of the roadway, stopped, and waited. An angry renegade called, "That ain't no fourteen head; what're you tryin' to do, get your womenfolk killed?"

Cap answered loudly. "These are only the horses we didn't have outfits for. The others are behind a building at the upper end of town—already rigged out."

"Lead 'em out where we can see 'em—all of them!"

Lee, no longer part of the conversation, went down a dogtrot, emerged in the east-side alley, and was hiking northward when he saw a number of women ahead.

Marta had brought them from Mex-town. Lupe Villaverde was slightly taller than most of them; her straight back and easy stride were all the marshal had to see to recognize her.

By the time he reached the north end of town, possemen were already moving out with the saddled animals. He strode past Marta to join them, when she gripped his arm and said, "No! You stay here!"

Lee would have shrugged off her grip if it hadn't been surprisingly strong. When he turned to speak, she spoke first.

"*Tonto!* They will kill you even if they don't shoot anyone else. You are the law."

He remained with the women, of which there were at least fifteen, mostly those who had fought raiders from inside Morales's cantina.

During the lull, when the fighting had shifted away from Mex-town, they'd had time to rest and wash and eat, as well as to prepare the dead. They had put the dead raiders on the ground beside a *jacal*. No one would have wanted them in a house, but they had done the customary things such as washing their faces with cold water, combing their hair, using brooms to brush their clothing.

One man they put slightly apart from the others. They had recognized him when he had been alive as the leader of the renegades.

While the women stood on the north side of the building at the extreme north end of town, there was very little talk. Like Marshal Custis, they were listening.

It was a while before Cap called attention to the saddled animals, and everyone, except perhaps the renegades, was pleased at the darkness. Several of the animals were bunched up and ready to explode. They were handled very prudently.

The renegade with the accent answered Cap. "They're too bunched up. Spread out so we can count them."

Cap and the men with him obeyed.

The same renegade called again, "All right. Now you take them back, have your women lead them down in front of the jailhouse."

Cap dutifully turned, jerked his head, and led the way back. As before, the fractious animals were inclined to act up, but the other animals walked steadily along; troublesome horses, and especially mules, were herd critters. Being left behind bothered them more than the things on their backs. They moved up among the other animals, still bunched up.

At the corner of the building, Cap mutely held out the reins of the lead horse and Marta took them. Cap looked—

and was—very troubled. Marta smiled up at him, placed a hand lightly on his arm. He stood aside as other women took other reins.

When Marta was ready, she led her horse into the roadway and turned southward. The only sound was of hooves against dusty *caliche* as hard as stone from years of travel.

Lupe and a graying woman passed Marshal Custis. Lupe looked at him from an expressionless face as he said softly in Spanish, "Whatever happens, don't go with them." Lupe smiled and passed by. The older woman looked sharply at Lee Custis, then she, too, moved ahead.

Cap waited until the procession was in the center of the road before saying, "Down the back alley. Follow me."

They followed him until he reached the saloon and halted to listen before pushing on again. When he stopped again they were roughly opposite the storekeeper's residence, but there was no nearby dogtrot, so they had to go a little farther southward until they were almost opposite Sommers's livery barn before they could work their way single-file between buildings toward the main road. Again, darkness favored them. Something else also did: the renegades had seen the horses coming. Every desperate raider had his full attention on the saddled animals.

Lee Custis used the six remaining bullets from his shell-belt to top up his handgun. As he worked, he watched Marta. She moved steadily but without haste, dark gaze fixed on the jailhouse and the residence of the storekeeper.

The silence was total except for the sound of slow-pacing hooves and a whisper of leather rubbing over leather.

A man yelled from the storekeeper's house. "Past the jailhouse toward the sound of my voice."

Marta neither increased her gait nor altered her course from the middle of the wide roadway.

A tight-wound raider cursed loud and long. He was not the only person in this night whose nerves were taut.

The harsh-voiced man yelled at Marta to veer closer to the west side of the roadway, which she did, while continuing to walk southward. The harsh-voiced man called again. "Closer, right up to the edge of the duckboards . . . Now stop. Don't move, and keep your hands in plain sight."

The women halted. Lee, Cap, and the men across the road scarcely breathed. Without any preliminary a howling dog sat back somewhere, pointed its head toward the moon, and made its mournful sound.

Hair stiffened at the back of the neck of just about everyone who heard. When the unsettling sound wailed off into silence, there was neither movement nor sound in Peralta until the harsh-voiced man swore, then addressed the women again.

"Each one of you move to the head of your animal and stand in plain sight with your hands at your sides."

It required a few minutes for this order to be obeyed, and when it was, the renegade gave another order. "Don't move. A couple of fellers is comin' out to make sure you don't. Stand real still an' don't talk."

In a dark doorway with another man, Juan Morales spoke softly. "That son of a bitch."

His companion's reply was less intense. "Wait, partner. Just wait. They got to be as sure as they can be, an' even after that, unless we're almighty careful, some women are going to be shot."

Two slinking figures materialized around the north side of the house, guns gripped and aimed. No one moved among the horse-holders until the renegades began feeling for weapons, then a girl cursed one and spat at him. He dropped her with his left fist, stepped past, and felt for weapons on the next woman.

The man next to Morales raised his handgun and cocked it. Juan pushed the gun away. The man turned, his eyes blazing, and said, "That was my sister."

Juan already knew that. "What did you tell me—wait, partner. I'll hold him while you cut his throat. Let the hammer down and don't move."

A watching raider from inside the storekeeper's house called to the searchers. "Put that tall one in front. I got a claim on her."

The searchers ignored the man who had called to them. When they came to Marta, she showed a death's-head smile and held her arms away from her body. One searcher went over her while the other one looked at the saddled animals and said, "Gawddammit, there's mules!"

As his companion stepped away from Marta, he growled. "Anything's better'n nothing, Charley."

"But a damned mule can't run like a horse."

"Then be sure you get a horse. Come on."

As they turned back toward the house, Winchester barrels appeared among the windows of the house, limned by weak starlight. It would have been adequate protection if the men in the house knew where to aim. There was nothing moving or clearly visible across the wide road.

A few minutes later, when the searchers were back inside, the harsh-voiced man gave another order. "Ladies, turn them animals so's you're on their far side. *Do it!*"

They obeyed, facing eastward toward the hidden men opposite the storekeeper's house. Lee watched and waited; regardless of how careful the harsh-voiced killer was—and Lee would have admitted the man was taking every precaution—the battle of Peralta was going to end soon, if for no other reason than that the people of Peralta were on the offensive.

There was a long hush. The men in hiding with a clear view of the house fidgeted. Cap Franklin was flat down at the south end of the house opposite the livery barn. Two other possemen were in the dogtrot, one belly-down, the other man kneeling behind him. One enterprising soul from Mex-town had climbed to the roof of the general store. His vantage point was excellent; men watching elsewhere at ground level would be unlikely to see the carbine barrel above. But shooting from a height like that, even with good visibility, was chancy at best.

The reason for the long delay was that the renegades were arguing. None of them were novices at raiding and killing, but nor were any of them experienced in the kind of siege their dead leader had left them in. Several were adamant about not walking out where the women and horses were waiting; they wanted the animals led around back to the alley. Others, wishing only to get as far from Peralta as fast as they could, voiced the opinion that with the women facing toward any hidden men of Peralta, the townsmen would not shoot for fear of hitting the women.

By the time the argument ended, a lantern-jawed, fox-faced outlaw had decided to make a run for it on his own. He slipped out of the house into the flowers, across there to the dark residences westerly. With open country shadowy but in sight, he sidled carefully close to the south side of a house. He stopped to lean and peer around, then, with his six-gun in one fist, he pressed close again. He was about to move when a thick arm came soundlessly through the open window holding something round.

The blow was hard enough to crack a skull. The fox-faced outlaw crumpled in a heap. A burly, thick woman of grim visage and unkempt gray hair leaned to make sure her rolling pin had done its work.

It had. She twisted to hoarsely whisper for someone behind her to dart out, tie the renegade's ankles and wrists, fetch his six-gun, and get back inside.

CHAPTER SIXTEEN

"Abajo! Abajo!"

DESPITE ALL THEIR efforts to outsmart the renegades, or at the very least match their slyness, the possemen had been effectively neutralized. None of them could fire without the unacceptable risk of killing a woman, and if that wasn't bad enough, there were two other considerations. At the first shot, the saddled animals would react in terror, knocking down or dragging the women who were holding the reins. The second consideration was that the raiders would return the fire: if the possemen didn't hit the women, the raiders would.

Juan Morales looked at his companion and rolled his eyes in despair, something the other man did not see; he was watching the girl who had been knocked down. She was standing with the others again, clutching the bridle reins of a mule.

The argument inside the house ended when the harsh-voiced individual used his cocked gun to gesture the opposition into silence. After that, Carl Haus looked from man to man, then said, "Where's Winton?"

A younger renegade, little more than a boy, answered. "Went out the back door. I seen him." He smiled bleakly at the older man. "How far's he gonna get without a horse?"

Haus glared before swinging his gaze to the others. He did not have the time or the inclination to brood over the men who were no longer with him.

He was a vicious killer with a string of wanted dodgers out on him from Missouri to Idaho. He had come as close to being Frank Bauman's second-in-command as anyone, and right now no one even came close to contesting his orders.

When the same youth said, "They're watchin' an' waitin', sure as hell," Haus crinkled his eyes into a deadly smile and replied, "Well, well, you're finally gettin' a little dry behind the ears. Of course they're out there. Why d'you think I made them women into targets."

The youth's reply was typical of him. "I don't like hidin' behind no skirts."

"You'll learn you got to do a lot of things if you want to stay alive. . . ."

Haus surveyed the dirty, unshaven, sunken-eyed men facing him and continued as though there had been no interruptions.

"Frank led us into this mess, an' for that I'd kill him if I could. . . . I figure our chances about fifty-fifty; they ain't goin' to fire at us until they think they might not hit their women—so each of you hoist a female behind the saddle, an' that should protect your backs, anyway. Don't let 'em get down, and run southward as hard as them animals can go."

The pair who had gone over the women for weapons exchanged a look. If they had to knock someone over the head, they were not going to end up with mules.

Haus hitched at his shellbelt, which was depleted and therefore much lighter than it normally would have been.

He jerked his head while scowling at a short, thick, older man. "Go look out there." As the stocky man moved away, Haus gave another order. "Make damned sure your weapons have a full load."

No one moved; every one of them had already done this. A renegade with a prominent Adam's apple bobbled it when he asked a question. "Where do we meet, afterwards?"

Haus smiled bleakly. "*If* we meet, it'll be at the rendezvous on Cedar Creek like it always was."

The short, older man returned. "The women are standin' out there like statues with them animals, back to the house like you told 'em to do."

"How about the men?"

"Awful dark out there, Carl. They got to be somewhere around, but I didn't see none of 'em."

"Go look in the alley."

Again, as the older man departed, Haus looked at his companions. It required no gift of second sight to realize he was looking at some of them for the last time. He cursed Frank Bauman again.

The older man returned to report that as near as he could make out, there was no danger.

Haus snorted. "You'll believe anythin' if you believe that, Lem. They're around, all around."

A vicious-faced youth said, "How long we goin' to stand here talking? I figure to be ten miles away by sunrise."

"Which way?" Haus asked. "Straight up or straight down? Take my word for it, kid—straight down."

The youth was evidently not afraid of Carl Haus. His reply was curt. "Then we'll be riding' together."

Another time this remark might have brought smiles. Not now in the dark, ransacked house with its lingering stench.

Haus hitched at his depleted shellbelt again. Several of the men watching him got faint frowns on their faces. To them the harsh-voiced man seemed to be hesitating out of fear.

All of them were afraid. Sure as hell is hot, some of them weren't going to make it. Maybe none of them would.

Haus approached a front window from the near side and leaned slowly until he could see the saddled animals and the women. He came back and said, in a harsh voice, "Let's go, an' the devil take the hindmost."

They were positioned behind the front door when the youth reached, opened the door, and moved into the opening with a hand on his leathered six-gun. Nothing happened. He was a perfect target, and nothing happened. He turned a sneering look at Haus and stepped outside.

The porch was higher than the path leading to the plankwalk and the horses. The youth left the porch moving a little stiffly. Carl Haus was next. Behind him, the others followed. The last man was the renegade who did not want to make his escape on a mule. His reasoning was sound this time too: with everyone in front, he was well protected. If a fight erupted, he would be the last one to be shot at.

One of the raiders moved toward the horse Lupe Villaverde was holding. He was the one who had called to the searchers that he wanted her when they left.

She blanched as he held forth a hand for the reins. She handed them to him, avoiding personal contact.

The others were also taking reins. The mean-faced youth got a big mule. He was not tall, and the mule was at least sixteen hands. To get astride, he would have to reach up with both hands.

The girl who had been knocked down by one of the searchers held out the reins to the thin outlaw with a prominent Adam's apple. He ignored her as he snatched the reins. His eyes probed eastward, where darkness concealed men with guns.

The women edged closer together as the renegades moved to mount. The raiders turned and snarled for the women to come back where the horses were.

The women moved a little closer to the men who were ready to mount. The man closest to Lupe Villaverde swept his arm toward her, but she was just beyond reach.

At that moment the others swung astride, and at once a harness horse and a pack mule broke in the middle. Neither was a riding animal. Neither could buck very well, but they tried. The horse bucked past Carl Haus and lighted out in a belly-down run toward open country.

The pack mule also bucked. Any good buckaroo could have ridden him—mules have straight backs with almost no spring in their spines. This mule bawled as it bucked. It, too, went southward. It was still doing its damnedest when Haus yelled for the others to run for it.

The renegade atop the fighting pack animal swerved, almost colliding with Haus when both he and his saddle sailed off the mule.

Marta watched. From the corner of her eye she saw men moving in shadows across the road. She yelled above the noise to the women around her. *"Abajo! Abajo!"*

The women dropped flat before the first blaze of gunfire lanced red from doorways and dogtrots, even from the roof of the general store.

The renegades rode, twisting to fire back. Targets were night-shadowed and moving. None of the raiders were hit until two men behind Haus, too excited to crouch low, were shot off their mounts north of the livery barn. One went off with both arms outflung. He sailed like a stricken bird, fell, and was trampled by other fleeing men. He felt nothing. The man on the rooftop had aimed at the middle of his back and had hit him in the back of the head.

The other man was punched violently forward when a large slug hit him in the back. He dropped his weapon, grabbed the saddle horn with both hands, and managed to hang on until he was abreast of the livery building, where an old man with a massive old rifle, which had a hexagonal barrel, took a long rest against the building and fired. His gun sounded like a cannon. This time the injured outlaw was almost lifted from the saddle and hurled sideways.

Marta got to her feet, neglecting the manured dust on her clothing to stand rigidly watching. The other women did the same.

It happened to several outlaws at about the same time: their horses ran out from under their saddles. The vicious-looking youth and Carl Haus were riding straight up in perfect balance, but men who had ridden off-balance or who had tried to twist to fire back came off their animals in tumbling falls, entangled and furiously threshing.

Lee, Cap, and the others shot at the men already beginning to fade in the southward darkness. The man above the store fired his Winchester empty and had to desist; the escaping handful of renegades were beyond six-gun range and within moments would be sheltered by darkness.

An angry voice near the lower end of town yelled for the unhorsed and entangled men to pitch their guns away. One of them fired three times in the direction of the voice, missing with all three shots. The old man in the livery barn had had time to reload his heavy rifle. He took a hand rest, aimed, and shot the wildly cursing outlaw who had hurled his handgun. As before, the impact of the lead slug the old gun fired literally lifted the outlaw and flung him sideways.

Several townsmen walked toward the center of the road and aimed downward at the unhorsed renegades.

The brother of the girl who had been knocked down looked among the fallen men until he found the one who had hurt her. He raised his six-gun and aimed from a distance of no more than fifteen feet. When he cocked the gun, the frantic raider rolled and tried to scramble clear.

Cap Franklin appeared from nowhere, struck the shooter's right arm with one big hand, grabbed cloth with the other hand, and flung the shooter aside so hard he stumbled and fell.

The young man's black eyes were murderous as he

started to rise. Juan Morales came from behind, grabbed his gun arm, and twisted it backward until the gun fell.

There were five badly shaken, dirty, rumpled renegades standing near the saddles they had used. Around them men of Peralta formed an armed ring. The raiders were ashen, hands over their heads.

Old Asa Flowers, leaning on his shot-out old buffalo rifle in the livery-barn doorway, spoke without haste or excitement. "Find horses, boys. Go after them that got away."

No one heeded Asa. There were no horses, and right at this moment they were concerned with prisoners. Lee gestured for the renegades to walk toward his jailhouse. Several townsmen went along. Lee herded the prisoners down to a cell and locked them in.

Lee returned to the roadway where the others were dragging the corpses away. Several saddleless horses returned to the lower end of town dragging reins. Not all horses had a homing instinct, but many horses who had been fed well and regularly in one place, did.

The smell of burnt powder was strong. There was no air stirring. It was still warm and would not turn cool for some hours yet, not until shortly before sunrise.

A few women appeared clutching shawls, seeking their men with terror in their hearts.

The women from Mex-town were across in front of the general store, watching, waiting for furiously beating hearts to return to normal.

Juan Morales eyed them from in front of the jailhouse. He started toward them. At the same time, Lee Custis came out and headed in that direction to express gratitude to the women and to say how relieved he was that none had been shot.

An older woman, sturdily built with awry gray hair and a stubborn set to her jaw, waggled a finger at Juan. "I watched you; you should get away from the cantina more . . . I watched you. Twice you shot your gun empty and did not hit any of them."

Juan glared but said nothing. The other women were grinning at him. Lupe Villaverde spoke to the marshal.

"It worked. I doubted that it would, but we were desperate, and God made it work."

Lee nodded at the beautiful woman. "What worked?"

Lupe Villaverde said, "Ask Marta."

Lee turned with raised eyebrows, silent and waiting. Marta reached down the back of her dress between the shoulders and drew forth a razor-sharp dagger with an old-fashioned engraved silver handle. She held it for Lee to see as she explained. "We brought knives with us. When we were told to take the horses and lead them down there, each one of us cut all but one strand of every cinch."

Marta returned the wicked-bladed knife to its leather sheath between her shoulder blades. "One strand would hold until they swung astride, but if an animal bucked or shied or if a rider rode too much to one side . . ."

Lee stood a moment eyeing the small woman with the tiger's heart. Then he laughed hard and long.

CHAPTER SEVENTEEN

A Mystery

NO ONE IN town was sure of the exact number of renegades who had managed to stay atop the running horses. It was thought to be somewhere between three and six. Old Asa Flowers said he had seen a youth and two other low-crouching raiders racing down the night.

He also told Lee Custis that if he had a horse he would go after them, that such vermin should not be left alive. But Asa had no horse; neither did anyone else until the night was sufficiently advanced to begin paling out with increasing chill, by which time other horses had drifted back to town, mostly without saddles. By then it was close enough to a new day for people to have enough to do without chasing outlaws who had at least a three-hour head start.

The womenfolk of Mex-town and Gringto-town mingled; pain and tears made clear that when serious trouble came, survival and cooperation were what mattered.

Several women refused to talk about their experiences. Some had experienced or witnessed pain, anguish, and humiliation at the hands of the raiders. Some had fought back.

A granite-jawed burly woman prodded an unsteady renegade toward the jailhouse, followed by her husband, a thin, timid-looking man. When she encountered Lee Custis, she roughly punched her unsteady prisoner forward.

"Here's another one for you," she told the marshal. "He tried to slip past the side of our house earlier. I hit him over the head." The woman's fiery glare lingered on the fox-faced renegade, whose head throbbed so much his eyes watered and his body trembled. "I hope," she said, "I cracked the son of a bitch's skull."

Her husband was embarrassed at her language and feebly smiled at Lee, who took the fox-faced prisoner into the jailhouse and locked him up with the others.

Marta and several other women, including Lupe Villaverde, had established a hospital of sorts in Kelly's saloon. There was no medical doctor closer than a hundred miles. Most of the injuries were less than serious.

While there was still a chill in the new day and before distant mountains emerged from their night-long gloom, Mike Kelly and Juan Morales rounded up four loose horses, took them down to the livery barn to be rigged out, and sent word by old Asa Flowers what they were doing.

By the time Lee arrived, they had found new reins for the ones frightened horses had stepped on and snapped off. They told Lee they needed two more men to join them in going after the raiders. They did not ask him to go along—someone was required in town to create as much order out of chaos as could be done—but Lee moved to the head of one horse, gathered the reins, and led the horse outside to be mounted. Asa Flowers did the same. He had parked his buffalo rifle somewhere and now had only an oversized, equally antiquated six-gun. He had no holster, so the weapon was shoved down the front of his waistband.

Kelly and Juan exchanged a glance. Juan shrugged and led his horse out front. Kelly followed, and until the four of them were below town, the animals warmed out, Kelly occasionally glanced at the old man without speaking. Asa caught him staring and said, "You got some objection, Mike?"

Kelly shook his head and thereafter concentrated on riding.

Regardless of how far ahead the fleeing outlaws were, they could be expected to be watching their back trail.

Lee pondered the alternative to the route they were taking. They could go either to the east or west of the coach road, and with prudence cover a lot of ground without being seen.

The problem was that they would then be unable to use shod-horse tracks to follow the renegades, and, giving the devil his due, these were not simply range riders they were hunting, these were men who had spent years avoiding being caught. Lee doubted that there would be a trick in the book those men did not know and would not use.

Old Asa made Lee's decision for him with a dry remark. "With a long head start we ain't goin' to run them down, Marshal. Not that kind; they'll change horses every chance they get. As long as men chase other men, they'll always be behind 'em."

Mike Kelly eyed the old man. "What's on your mind?" he asked.

"Got to sidle around them someway."

Kelly nodded sourly. "How do we do that without wings?"

Asa showed no irritation when he replied. "We do the same thing they're doing. We steal fresh horses as we go along, and we ride 'em into the ground. When they rest, we don't; when they bed down for a couple hours' sleep, we don't."

Kelly eyed the frail-seeming old man. Asa Flowers did not seem strong enough for a two-hour ride, let alone the kind of ride he was proposing. Kelly looked away, saw Juan watching him, and rolled his eyes.

Lee swung west off the coach road, loped on an angling southwesterly course until the road was a distant ribbon, then aimed southward again. Out here the land had occasional patches of cover, but generally it was more or less flat and open. Visibility was good; it was too early for heat haze to appear.

It bothered Lee, the farther they rode, that if the renegades left the coach road somewhere along their way, Lee and his companions would not know it and would be riding southward while their prey might be heading easterly, or maybe even back northward.

He resolved this by asking Juan Morales to return to the road and follow the fresh shod-horse tracks. If they branched off somewhere, Juan was to stand in his stirrups and wave his hat.

After Juan left, the others continued southward. Once, they saw a distant clutch of buildings, but to go that far out of their way for fresh animals would use up more time than Lee wanted to spare.

They saw no more signs of cow outfits until they were miles along southward and came over a land swell with a big yard dead ahead. It had bleached log buildings and shade. A man appeared in the yard, watching their approach.

Two more men appeared, one from the main house, the other from a huge old log barn, to stand wide-legged, watching. Lee led his companions close and raised his right hand palm forward. Then the man on the veranda of the main house came down to join the man in front of the barn.

The afoot men walked over to a tierack. They were gray, weathered, and wrinkled. One was as lean as a beanstalk, the other more fleshy. The heavier man waited until the riders halted, then muttered to the lean man, "It's the marshal from Peralta."

His companion nodded and loosened a little. He spoke thoughtfully. "Seems you was right; there must be somethin' wrong up yonder."

Lee drew rein, nodded, and wasted no time asking the

men if they could remount the marshal and his companions. The fleshy man was blunt. "Who you after, Marshal?"

"Raiders attacked Peralta. Several got away. We need fresh animals to continue the chase."

The fleshy man told his ranch hand, "Get 'em horses, Quentin."

After the lean old man departed, his employer gestured. "Get down, gents. While we're waitin' you could tell me about the raid."

Lee told him, with an occasional confirmation from Mike Kelly. Only Asa was silent; after a few moments, he went down through the barn where the elderly rangeman was catching horses in an outback pole corral. Asa watched; as the other old man was leading three horses out, he said, "We'll need four, partner. We got a feller over on the coach road readin' sign."

Without a word, the other man handed Asa the shanks and went after another horse. As he was leading this one out, he asked how bad the raid had been. Asa told him in his dry way of speaking. The rangeman took one of the shanks, but before leading off up through the barn he said, "How many got clear?"

Asa guessed. "Maybe three, maybe a few more."

The cowboy thought a moment. "Wouldn't have been maybe eight or ten, would it?"

Asa shook his head.

"Well, I went out this mornin' to set the crew to work, an' on my way back I seen about ten or twelve strangers crossing from the northwest. I watched 'em pass from a stand of trees; they was armed to their gullets, ridin' wearyin' horses."

Asa slowly shook his head. He was curious, but not that many had escaped and they had gone due south. He led off up through the barn. "Couldn't be the same bunch, but I'd sure keep my eyes open if I was you. Raiders like isolated outfits like this."

Out front, the men from Peralta removed saddles and bridles. There was a little desultory conversation during this time. The fleshy man had already told Lee about the party of strangers his hired man had seen. Lee was puzzled but, like Asa, was of the opinion it might be more raiders. The damned country seemed to be full of them.

As they swung back astride and told the cowman they'd return his livestock as soon as they could, he wished them luck. They thanked him and left the yard riding westward. They wanted to find Juan Morales.

They found him heading toward them at an easy lope. When he came up, Kelly flung him the reins of the fourth horse. As Juan went about off-saddling, then resaddling, he told them the sign never deviated, it went straight south.

Lee asked if he had seen a party of riders. Juan shook his head, gathered the reins, and mounted. Asa was of the opinion that if that beanpole back in the yard had seen those riders coming from the northwest, there was a good chance they had not gone as far as the coach road but had turned in another direction.

Unless they had gone back the way they had come, which seemed unlikely, and they hadn't come down to the coach road where Juan would have seen them, then there was only one way they could have gone—southward.

They were bothered by the presence of that many heavily armed men somewhere around. Lee asked Mike Kelly to ride westerly, see if he could find any tracks going southward. As Kelly loped away on his fresh horse, Asa looped his reins, fished forth a lint-encrusted plug, gnawed off a corner, returned the tobacco to a pocket, leaned to expectorate, and finally spoke.

"Country's gettin' a mite crowded."

Juan shrugged. He was anxious to move along, and turned his new mount with Lee on one side and Asa on the other side. They did not return to the coach road; they paralleled it from a decent distance.

The nearest town southward was a village called Leesville. It was a way station for the stage company and had no more than five huts and a big old log main structure beside several corrals.

The station came into sight in the distance. As they approached, Juan mentioned that the corral was full of horses. Maybe the fugitives had swept past and maybe they hadn't.

As they came closer, a large, bearded man stood in the yard watching them. The big man had no shellbelt or holstered weapon. He did not look as though he would need them under ordinary circumstances.

He boomed a loud welcome to the men from Peralta when they were still a fair distance out, which made Juan shake his head as he said, "He don't sound like a man who's had his remuda raided."

The big man saw Asa, and smiled widely as the horsemen came up and halted. "Thought you was dead," he said. "Y'ought to be, Asa. Ain't decent for a feller to live as long as you have."

The old man grinned from his saddle and returned the greeting. "Mister Barling, I do like you do. I stay clear of any kind of work so's I can live a long time."

Barling roared with laughter as he invited the men to alight. Lee remained in the saddle as he asked Barling if he had seen several riders heading south.

The big man nodded. "Last evening, about five or six riders passed without stoppin'. . . . But when I was out back earlier I seen a fair-sized band of riders headin' south, out west a ways."

Lee asked, "About ten of them?"

Again, the big man nodded. "That's right, ten or so of 'em." He considered Juan, Asa, and the marshal briefly. "You after them gents? If you are, an' ain't got a Gatling gun to even up the odds, I'd say you don't have a chance in hell. Them lads was armed with everything a man could carry. . . . What'd they do?"

Lee was baffled and only shrugged off the big man's question as he raised his rein hand. "I got no idea. They're not the ones we're after," he said, nodded, and led off.

Asa, the last man to ride past the large individual, leaned from the saddle and said, "Raiders hit Peralta, killed folks, tore things up. Big mob of them. It was a hell of a fight while it lasted, Mister Barling. A couple of 'em made a run for it. They're somewhere ahead."

The big man stood watching Lee and his friends break over into a little lope on their southward trail. He'd worried about marauders for years, had his log main-building built with loopholes in the walls, and had racked up two rows of rifles, carbines, shotguns, and pistols.

Ordinarily, raiders would not bother such a poor place as a way station, except for one thing: horses. It had not happened this time. Evidently, the fleeing men felt the horses under them would do for a while.

Lee returned to the road where the sign was still fresh and going southward. He turned back westerly, hoping watching renegades had not seen their sortie.

Mike Kelly rejoined them. Asa and Kelly mumbled back and forth. Kelly did not like the idea of another band of raiders being somewhere around. Asa reset his hat, chewed, and spat before answering. "You ain't goin' out one second before you're supposed to an' not one second after you're supposed to."

Kelly turned, scowling, as he stood in his stirrups to squint ahead.

After a while, Juan dismounted to get a closer look at some tracks. Lee asked what he saw.

Juan straightened slowly, looking at the lawman. "I don't like this," he said. Then he returned to studying a lot of shod-horse tracks.

Asa shuffled eastward a dozen yards before calling to the others. "They left the road and was comin' in this direction. Three of them, which was our raiders sure as hell." He walked slowly back until he reached the others and halted, frowning. "What the hell . . . They come together." The old man raised his eyes, peering westward. "Now, it couldn't have been them other fellers escaped too, could it? *Ten?* Naw, it can't be."

Kelly pointed to the marked ground. "Maybe it was other raiders; maybe they met 'em and rode west with 'em." Kelly did not like this at all. "That'll make thirteen of them bastards. . . . Lee?"

The marshal spat, reset his hat, and squinted westerly, the direction the riders had gone. "There's something . . . Put it together; those riders was seen by that cowman's rider real early. The feller at the stage stop saw them too, riding south, an' that was early this morning too." He paused to glance around. "Whoever they are, they wouldn't have known those three renegades was runnin' for it."

Asa contradicted that. "Sure they knew. They had to know; otherwise they wouldn't have been down here to meet the raiders. Question is, Lee . . . We're four, they outnumber us maybe three to one. You want to die today?"

Kelly didn't. "Couple of us can go back for more men while the other two tracks them fellers."

Juan Morales did not want to be one of the men to make the long ride back. "All four of us track them, careful as Indians. See what we're up against. Then, if we got to, someone can go for help."

Kelly rolled his eyes but said nothing. They turned westerly, with the sun sliding off in the same direction.

CHAPTER EIGHTEEN
A New Trail

THE SIGN WAS easy to read and even easier to follow, but Asa waited until they were a mile or so westerly, in the direction of rougher, more timbered country, to make a statement consistent with knowledge derived from at least fifty years' experience.

"Ain't ten, lads. It was twelve of 'em before they met our raiders."

Juan shrugged. Riding after twelve killers was no different from risking his life going after fifteen. Mike Kelly rode with a closed-down expression and cautious, wary eyes on the country ahead. Where they had come from there was precious little timber; more brush and grass. They were following sign leading directly into some trees. After they had covered another mile, he said, "We spent the mornin' ridin' so's they wouldn't see us. Now then, gents, look up yonder. If anyone's watchin' an' I'd bet my life they are, we're ridin' right down their damned rifle barrels."

No one disputed this, but since the tracks they were following led toward the distant trees, without cover until they got over there, they kept on riding, mostly silent, very watchful.

A very faint scent of dust still clung to the motionless air where the riders they were seeking had passed.

Asa asked if the others had ever been in this country

before, knew what the answer would be, and as soon as he got it, raised his right hand to stop. "I'll scout ahead," he told them. "Maybe they got a watcher out, but I doubt it, unless they seen us crossin' open country. In any case, I'll snoop ahead."

Asa walked his horse forward around and among the huge fir trees.

They could not ride together as they'd done up until now; the huge trees were too closely spaced.

There was still sunlight out in the open, but among the old trees, there was perpetual gloom. The farther they tracked, the deeper they got into the forest, and the more pine and fir sap scent blocked out all other odors.

Day-long heat, which had not actually been bad this day, hadn't penetrated where they were riding in several hundred years. It was cool, shadowy, and because generations of fallen needles made the ground spongy, their horses made no sound.

For a long while there was no sign of the old man. When he did appear, wraithlike, his expression was different, no longer tough and closed.

Leaning a little but with both hands atop the horn, he said, "There's a clearin' up yonder, maybe forty, fifty acres. Most likely an old burn, but it's got good grass an' a little creek."

Kelly was a direct individual. "Are they out there?" he asked.

Asa nodded, still almost smiling. "They ain't fools, I can tell you that. They got a little supper fire goin'. Not a hint of smoke. All bone-dry wood."

"How many?" asked Marshal Custis.

"Fifteen. An' they're keepin' their horses close so ain't no chance of slitherin' through the grass and settin' them afoot."

Asa dismounted to rest his animal's back, spat out a cud that had lost all flavor, and blew out a long breath as he looked westerly toward the distant clearing he could not see for trees.

"It's goin' to be directly," he said, still looking in the direction of the clearing. He swung his attention to Marshal Custis. "I don't see no way to do much unless we wait for dark an' run off their horses."

The other men also dismounted. Lee considered, eyed the overhead merging stiff tops of giant trees, and said, "Hide the horses. If they're in the open an' if we stay in the timber . . ."

Asa led them northward a quarter mile, where they left the horses. He then led them on a diagonal course among the trees and the last hundred yards or so cautioned them about silence.

The clearing seemed a far distance to men on foot lugging Winchesters. In fact, it was a tad over half a mile. They saw sunlight reaching the ground before they actually arrived close to the ancient burn.

A horse whinnied. The men lazing around the fire out across the meadow jerked alert. One man got to his feet, tugged his hat low, and with a Winchester in his hand strode northward across the clearing. He went in the direction the whinnying horse was looking.

Around the supper fire the other men, mostly with their backs to the men from Peralta, sat down atop dry, fragrant needles. They did not act worried, but the ones who had been lounging did not return to that position. One man fed the fire; another stranger had meat turning on a green-wood spit. The aroma made Mike Kelly's mouth water. Lee looked at Juan, rolled his eyes, and with his head raised, inhaled deeply. Morales smiled understanding; none of them'd had a thing to eat since before they had left town.

Asa eased back as the prowling man disappeared among the trees. He rose and turned in the same direction. Lee, Kelly, and Morales watched him depart. The whinnying horse in the clearing had undoubtedly scented-up the tied horses among the northward trees.

Asa moved like a shadow from tree to tree, smiling again, old eyes slitted and willing. His step was springy, his heart was holding to a steady cadence in its dark place.

He edged slightly to his left, hoping to see the man from the fire. Asa had one advantage: he knew the other man was up here, and although it had been years since he'd done anything like this, it came back to him easily.

He paused often to listen. This was what eventually permitted him to get a bearing. He changed course again, due north, this time in the direction of a man's spurs.

There was no bird song, no scuttling of small critters; the forest was still, silent, waiting.

Asa got close enough to see the horses and watched them. When their attention was suddenly toward the west, Asa moved beside a rough-barked old sugar pine and leaned as he gently lifted the horse pistol.

The man appeared, stopped dead still at sight of four saddled horses, seemed rooted to the ground as he stared where he probably had expected to see one stray horse.

He was thin, black-haired and black-bearded, not young and not old. Asa raised the old pistol and slowly cocked it. *That* sound traveled.

The dark man did not start or turn to run; he very slowly twisted from the waist, looking around. His gaze raked Asa's tree and came back to the horses. He was not challenged, had seen no one, but without question knew what that cocking sound meant. He grounded his Winchester, leaned on it, and waited.

Asa spoke without showing himself. "Let go the carbine, mister." When the man had obeyed, Asa gave another order. "Get flat down on your belly an' shove your hands as far ahead as you can. Keep your face down."

Again the lean man obeyed. Only when he thought the

bodiless voice would show did he move his head. Asa clucked at him. "Face in the needles an' keep it there."

The lean man obeyed, but he had recovered from surprise, from shock, and spoke against the ground. "If you'n your friends is after money . . . There's a lot of us an' only four of you."

Asa moved among trees until he was behind the prone man before stepping into sight. He waited, but the stranger did not attempt to peek around. Asa went up, kicked the Winchester away, shoved a cold muzzle against the man's neck, and lifted away his six-gun. He then stepped back, considered his prisoner, and was about to ask questions when somewhere southwesterly a man shouted.

"Walt? Anythin' out there?"

Asa stepped close and swung the long-barreled old pistol. The young scout arched up off the ground and fell back as slack as a dead man.

Asa dragged Walt southward away from the area of their tethered horses. He could not avoid leaving a trail a blind man could follow.

If he owned a hundred dollars he would gladly have given it just to have Walt walk in a direction other than the one he had walked. Discovery of their horses was a disaster, and he'd had to compound it by knocking the man senseless. His friends, already alert, would worry when Walt did not return.

Where Asa left him, arms lashed behind his back using the stranger's own bandanna, and using his trouser belt to lash his legs at the ankle, he would be easy to find by anyone who came looking for him, saw the tethered saddled horses, saw the drag marks and followed them.

Asa hastened back to the others. They listened to what he had done and gazed at each other. Soon, the men in the clearing would start hunting for their companion. It would not take long to find him. When that was done, they would have a reason to do what the men of Peralta had planned to do to them: set them afoot.

Mike Kelly groaned and turned to watch the men in the clearing. So far they were still sitting out there. They were probably hungry, but that was not likely to prevent them from starting a hunt when their friend did not return.

Lee said, "We better get hid up by the horses."

Mike Kelly, who still did not like the odds, grumbled something about if they'd used their damned heads they'd have come out here with a full-size posse. Maybe the others agreed, but it was too late now.

They skirted as close as they dared in order to be able to watch the men at the supper fire. So far, none of them had left the area.

Asa led them to where Walt was still unconscious, then from there to one side of the drag marks until they could see their tethered animals. Asa felt ashamed for what he had done, but if he hadn't done it, and Walt had got back to warn his friends at the fire . . .

"Walt! Come on, meat's gettin' cold."

Juan Morales said they should move the horses, hide them better. The others agreed, and while Asa kept watch they led their animals farther back and southward. Juan smiled as they retied them. It was close to dusk, which would make the gloom among the trees even thicker and darker; no one could tracks their horses in darkness.

Kelly was worried about the unconscious man. "They ain't idiots; they'll know someone's out here."

Of course, he was right. Lee motioned for them to return to the area of the unconscious man. There were now fourteen of them by his calculations. Even in the open it would have been difficult for four men to successfully throw down on fourteen men.

A shout carried among the trees. "Walt! Come on back. You don't have to watch. You can set here an' eat while we're doin' it."

Lee and Juan exchanged a look. Apparently, the man Asa had coldcocked had not wanted to watch something. It did not matter what it was, as long as his companions thought he was staying away from the camp deliberately.

Juan wagged his head. Miracles were rare, but this was sure one.

CHAPTER NINETEEN

An Unexpected Encounter

FROM THEIR HIDING place, the Peralta men watched the men at the supper fire eat, speaking a little around mouthfuls of food. A thick-shouldered man whose back was to the edge of the clearing spoke in a clear voice. "Danged fool. He never had no stomach for this."

Another man challenged that remark. "Well, don't nobody really *like* it, do they? I been on plenty rides with Walt. He's a good man."

That seemed to end the conversation until they were through eating. When dusk began to settle, a short, burly man arose sucking his teeth. He went over where the saddles were upended and brought back several lariats. Not a word was said as he returned and sat down with the lariats. A quavery, young-sounding man said, "We told you, we didn't have nothin' to do with that. Me an' Carl an' Lem wasn't even in the country up there."

The next speaker was instantly recognized by the men from Peralta as the one who had been the raiders' spokesman. "The kid's tellin' you the gospel truth."

One of the other men said, "You wasn't at Peralta either, was you, you lyin' son of a bitch."

There was a period of silence again.

The stocky man looked around, saw his companions wiping fingers, and grunted as he shoved up to his feet with the lariats over one arm.

145

The youth choked, coughed violently until the harsh-voiced man thumped him on the back several times, then stopped coughing and cried out, "You can't do it, for Chrissake! You got to hand us over to the law. What you're fixin' to do makes you as bad as—"

"Shut up," the man with the lariats said scornfully. "Stand up!" Several of the other men rose, but the three at the lower end of the circle did not move.

A graying man the others called Elam jerked his head in the direction of the man holding the lariats, who turned and walked directly toward the fringe of the forest beyond which the men of Peralta were hidden by several tiers of huge old trees. In the midst of the crowd were three men walking stiffly, prodded when they faltered by men in back.

Lee Custis would have crept farther back, but movement would have been detected even in shadows. He and his friends became as still as stones.

The man called Elam stopped among the first trees and scanned them, as did his companions, until the stocky man carrying lariats spoke in a calm, businesslike voice.

"Them three side by side with strong lower limbs."

No one disputed; none of them wanted to prolong this. Carl Haus had very bright eyes, high color in his cheeks, and wet lips. He put on a show of courage by saying, "Them limbs is too high. There's better ones behind—"

"Shut your gawddamned mouth!" the man with the lariats said, glaring. He looked at the man called Elam. "We got to bring up three horses, unless we figure to do this by manpower."

An older man in the gathering shouted, "Pull 'em up! By Gawd, for what I lost I want to feel my arms pullin' them up."

Two men accepted ropes from the stocky man, and all three of them went to work wrapping hang-knots. The stocky man finished first and held his aloft to test it.

"Take your time," another man said. "It goes against my grain to get it over quick; let 'em have a taste of what they give others. Hoist 'em up an' let 'em down a few times, then haul 'em up for the buzzards to find."

The heretofore silent man standing beside Carl Haus finally spoke, and because it was the first time since the riders had caught the three of them west of the coach road, the others stopped what they were doing and listened.

"Somethin' I'd like someone to explain. When we turned off that coach road headin' west—how come you to be out there waiting?"

Elam replied in the same calm and quiet tone of voice the question had been asked.

"After you sons of bitches raided our town up north, me an' Charley Bennett, the feller with the lariats, tracked you after telling folks back in Aromanches to get up a posse and follow after us.

"We tracked you to hell an' gone west, then down in the direction of Peralta. We knew what you'd do down there because of what you done to our town, so me an Charley rode hard back until we found the others. They was a long way back. We rode close enough to know there wasn't no way we could ride into Peralta without maybe gettin' shot by both sides; anyway, the fightin' was dwindling. So we rode back out a ways and done some figuring. You wasn't goin' to escape north, not back toward our town. You most likely was goin' to use the coach road south, but just in case you went east, we crept close enough to see you leave town. When you started south, we rode the same direction, only faster and harder until we was well around you with daylight comin'. We rode parallel to you a mile or so, then you decided to throw off pursuit by turnin' west. You know the rest of it. We come up out of a gully in a long line, caught you hands down, and waited for you to start shootin'. Our intention was to riddle you until your own mothers wouldn't recognize you. But you murdering cowards just sat out there." Elam paused to look at the men with the ropes, and nodded.

No one spoke. The stocky man named Bennett had to make three casts before he got his rope over the big low branch.

When the ropes were ready, some men held the youth while two others lowered the rope and snugged up the big knot under his right ear.

Another man prodded the quiet raider while someone else lashed his hands behind his back with a pigging string. When he was urged forward, he walked without missing a step or faltering in his stride. When they lowered the rope, he obligingly leaned his head slightly to one side to make the adjustment easier. His face was expressionless, his body relaxed.

One of the men from Aromanches surreptitiously crossed himself for this one.

The last man to be placed beneath a low limb was Carl Haus. He did not tilt his head for the knot, but he grinned wolfishly at the men around him in unsteady firelight as he said, "You gawddamned bunch of churchgoin', money-stealin', whining sons of bitches. I'll be waitin' for you in hell."

Elam nodded. All hands moved toward Carl Haus. He gave them a fight up to the end. The next man to be pulled high was the quiet raider. He, too, flopped and gyrated. Only the youth didn't. He seemed to slide out of life without any sense of a need for remaining.

Firelight made the scene less macabre than frightening. It glowed against bloating faces, swaying bodies, unkempt men in filthy clothing who were choking to death.

Lee called out to the Aromanches riders and identified himself. They welcomed the Peralta men, knowing that Peralta had suffered as their own town had.

Back through the timber, Asa rose and went purposefully back where he had left the unconscious man. Walt was conscious when he arrived, sitting propped against a tree with watering eyes and a sick headache. Asa wordlessly knelt and removed the bindings. The man raised both hands to his face and moaned.

Asa hunkered and waited. It was a long wait. One of the unknowns about hitting someone over the head with a gun had to do with the thickness of a skull. Evidently, in this case it had not been very thick. The stranger seemed befuddled.

Asa stood up, hoisted the ailing man to his feet, and half-carried him down where his companions from Peralta and the men from Aromanches were mingling. When Asa arrived with the man he had coldcocked, the others looked without making a move to help, so Asa eased the stranger to the ground and stood over him. The men from Aromanches already knew from Lee what had happened to Walt. The stocky individual named Bennett told Asa, "I'll go get the whiskey."

The next morning, it took an hour for the strangers to strike their camp and assist the possemen from Peralta in lashing the corpses of the raiders over saddles, arms and heads dangling on one side, legs and feet dangling on the opposite side. What required the most time was fashioning cinches out of rope to replace the ones cut by the women of Mex-town, which had held this far but could not be relied upon to hold much longer, particularly on saddles over which limp dead men were tied.

Everyone sat a horse except the dead men. Asa took the lead position back through the darkness among huge trees, taking his time.

From the beginning there had been reason for haste, but no more.

There was also very little talk, not entirely because the crowd of armed men was tired, sore from horsebacking and the lynching, but also because those three flopping corpses among them inhibited conversation. Death, deserved or not, touched every man's consideration of being mortal, something it would not have done otherwise for considerable periods of time. Men understood the inevitability while simultaneously ignoring it during their everyday existence in favor of such things as ambition, desires, their labor, and their hopes. What now flopped soundlessly among them as they rode in the direction of the distant coach road was not the miracle of life, but the mystery of death.

CHAPTER TWENTY
Another Day

TIRED MEN ON weary horses passed like phantoms down out of trees to open country. They turned north at the coach road. The roadway was dimly visible in the cold early morning.

When they reached it and heard a heavy wheeled vehicle passing southward, Juan said, "Dawn coach."

They rode a considerable distance before Elam drew rein as he said, "We'll leave you gents here. We can make better time across country."

That was about all the leave-taking involved, an announcement and nodding heads. Lee was riding stirrup with Mike Kelly as they resumed their way. Behind them, Asa and Juan minded the led horses. Kelly glanced back several times; Asa Flowers was erect in the saddle, white stubble on his face, hooded old eyes as clear as springwater.

They stopped only once to dismount and rest the animals.

Some hours later, they reached town and angled to go up the westerly alleyway where they would not be noticed until after they had got rid of the half-curled stiff corpses. They put them side by side in the wagon shed behind and north of the livery barn, and were watched by horses lined up along their corrals, ears forward with interest.

Kelly and Juan left. Asa stood watching the marshal as

he said, "After I've got somethin' to eat, I'll trail the horses back down yonder to that cowman who lent 'em to us."

Lee was bone-weary. "Get some sleep," he told the old man. "Plenty of time to do that later."

Asa grinned. "When you're as old as me you'll learn something—old men need darned little sleep, but they like to doze a lot. See you when I get back."

Lee shrugged and trudged up the alley to the rear of his jailhouse, went inside, barred the door after himself, dropped his hat on his desk, went to open the front door, and noticed the cooking smell of breakfast fires throughout town. Tired as he was, his stomach grumbled.

There was a townsman over in front of the café sucking his teeth. Lee closed the door at his back and went like a moth to a flame in the direction of the beanery.

When he entered, there were only two diners at the counter. They and the caféman stared. Lee went to the counter. "Coffee to start with," he told the caféman. "Then a double setup of breakfast steak, spuds, and more coffee."

The caféman did not move; he frowned slowly. In an acidy tone of voice he said, "In case you're interested, Marshal, I been stoking the bellies of them smelly, bellyachin' prisoners of yours while you was gone. A man'd think you'd have made some kind of arrangements about that."

Lee regarded the indignant man across the counter. "Remember, Peralta was raided. We went after the ones that run off."

The caféman barely inclined his head. "Yeah, I know. The whole town knows. . . . Did you get 'em?"

Lee's irritation was increasing. "When you're not too busy," he said sourly, "go look in Foggy's wagon shed. They aren't pretty an' they're stiffer'n ramrods. . . . Yes, we got 'em. . . . Double ration of steak and spuds and set the coffeepot where I can reach it."

The other diners rose en masse, put coins beside their

plates, and departed for the livery. The caféman watched this exodus, then went to his cooking area after placing a large mug of black java before the marshal. Lee took the coffee with him as he went to stand at the roadway window. Peralta still showed signs of battle; what amazed the lawman was how much cleaning up had been accomplished since he'd left town.

The caféman returned with a hot platter. His tone was grudgingly different when he said, "Damn near filled up the cemetery yestiddy evening." He waited until Lee was seated again before adding more. "That's a mean an' stinkin' lot in your cells. There's talk the army'll be along to take 'em off your hands."

Lee listened, ate, swilled coffee, and ate more. The caféman continued in his more or less normal tone of voice. "You know that old man in Mex-town who died just before the raid? Well, I'm not sure whether it's his daughter or granddaughter, but her and a real pretty little dark woman from down there—they set up a hospital in Kelly's saloon." The caféman's eyes twinkled sardonically. "Mike'll like that."

Lee smiled around a mouthful of steak and potatoes.

Six grim-faced townsmen appeared at the café. After one look at their faces, the caféman went quickly to his kitchen and stayed there.

The spokesman of the group was a jowly, heavy man named Curtis Bledsoe. He did not live in town, he was a cowman, but he owned several buildings in Peralta. Lee nodded toward him as he eyed the others. They had one thing in common: balky expressions.

The jowly man wasted no time. "Marshal, them men in your jailhouse . . ."

Lee nodded for the other man to continue, which Bledsoe did with a tougher sound to his voice. "They're murderers an' worse. What they done to folks can't never be excused or forgot."

Lee nodded again, this time with his coffee cup in hand.

"We went an' talked to them through the bars last night. There's a sick one in there, and there's one feller in there, a big mouthy feller, brave as hell with the bars between him an' us. He ain't one whit remorseful."

Lee guessed which prisoner that was and sipped coffee waiting for the rest of it.

"Marshal, we just heard you hung them three you run down southwest of town."

Lee spoke for the first time. "I didn't hang anyone. Neither did the men with me."

"Well, we just come from down there, an' they sure-Gawd been hung."

Lee explained what had happened.

This was the first anyone in Peralta knew about the posse riders from the town northwest of Peralta being this far south. They were surprised, but not at all surprised concerning the purpose of those men; nor did they show anything but approval over what had been done.

"Well, some of us," Bledsoe said, "had a meetin' last night. We concluded that's what should be done with them sons of bitches in your jailhouse, an' it's a relief to know you feel the same way."

Lee rose, counted out silver for his meal, and placed it beside his plate before facing the jowly man again.

"Up yonder where that lynching took place there was four of us and twelve of them. I had to decide whether to maybe get us killed or let the lynching take place.

"Down here it's different. They'll hang for sure, but the law'll do it, we won't."

For seconds there was not a sound as the jowly man's expression subtly altered, became closed and cold. He turned, jerked his head, and led his companions out of the café.

Before Lee could cross the road to look in on his prisoners, the caféman stopped him at the door. "You're makin' a mistake," he exclaimed as Lee turned back in the doorway. "Them scum killed and tortured, robbed and beat folks. If they'd been able, they'd have burnt the town. All you're talkin' about is feedin 'em and babyin' them until a judge can get down here, an' ain't a soul in Peralta who'll agree with that. They did their damnedest to destroy us. We don't need no circuit-rider to judge them for that, Marshal. We already done that!"

Lee lingered in the doorway, gazing at the man behind the counter. He was fed now, and he was too tired to argue. He nodded, and walked out into the sunshine.

He hesitated between going to his room and sleeping for a week, or going up to Kelly's place. It was on the way, so he went up to the saloon. The first person he saw was old Henry Poole, who was lying on a cot. There were other beds and other injured people. Lupe and Marta faced him from the middle of the room.

He smiled. "You organized this, Marta?"

She shrugged without smiling. "It had to be done. There are others at their homes. We look after them too."

Lee smiled at Lupe Villaverde. She smiled back before turning aside when an injured man asked for water. The women from both parts of town were working together to answer a common need.

Henry Poole said, "You caught 'em an' hanged 'em?"

Lee went to a small stool beside the cowman's cot and sat down, but did not answer the question. Henry Poole's color was good, and his eyes were bright. Lee grinned at him. "How come you aren't dead?"

The old cowman grinned back. "Well, now, sonny, a man can't always succeed in what he tries to do. Them ladies wouldn't let me." Henry's smile faded. "Lee, I was in Morales's saloon when it was attacked. I'm here to tell you I never seen men fight any better'n those women. That little one, Marta, by Gawd I'd never want her against me. She's been everywhere doin' everything. Why she just don't drop I'll never know. . . . You know her husband?"

"Frank? I've known him for years."

"Well, you know him better'n I do. Next time you see him, tell him ain't a man alive deserves a woman as good as her."

Marta crossed to his side. She leaned close and kissed old Henry on his beard-stubbled cheek, then straightened back and said, *"Gracias."*

Lee took her to the doorway and outside. He asked about casualties. She surprised him; not many townsfolk had been killed, although quite a few had been injured.

As she talked, he noticed a subtle change in her expression. She looked different than he had ever seen her look: bitter, cold, and fierce. When she saw him watching, she smiled at him.

"The town will heal," she told him. "Faster maybe than the people . . . especially the women." Her smile faded, to be replaced with that cold look again. "You look worn out. We can talk later. Oh, people worried, I meant to tell you, especially one person." She nodded back toward Lupe.

She left him standing out there.

He went to his room, shed filthy clothing, and dropped atop the bed. If someone had fired a cannon outside his window, he would not have heard it.

Through the day people continued to work at re-creating order. There was little they could do about bullet holes, but in time they would be patched over.

Actual damage to the town was much less extensive than people had expected. Dead raiders were buried with other casualties in the village cemetery on the easterly outskirts of town. One renegade in particular went into his grave not only unblessed but spat upon. Frank Bauman.

Mike Kelly did not react to his saloon's being turned into a hospital, as the caféman had thought he would. Later, he might complain a little. He went home and to bed. Juan

Morales did, too, but not until he had stood in the middle of his cantina looking at the scars and the damage.

He was leaving through the smashed doorway, paused to gaze at a muddy place where skid marks showed how a dead horse had been dragged away, when Cap Franklin came up. Juan flapped his arms. "It is ruined. Everything . . . Look in there."

Cap had already looked. Without a word he fished forth a fat pad of folded money and tucked it into Morales's pocket. Still silent, he then strode in the direction of Gringo-town.

Juan remained in place, watching the large man reach the alley and pass up through a dogtrot before he removed the money, counted it, counted it a second time, and looked westward again. But there was no sign of Cap.

Some of the greenbacks were stuck together, something Juan ignored; he now had enough money to restock his cantina, with enough left over for a new door.

He knew Cap Franklin, had known him a long time; they had never been close friends, but they had been friends. Juan repocketed the money.

Standing nearby under the shade of an ancient canvas texas, an old man spoke quietly in Spanish. "He gave you money, Juan?"

"Yes. A lot of money. I didn't know he was a rich man."

The old man eased down on a shaded bench. "I don't know whether he is a rich man or not, but I *do* know about that money he gave you. It is dry now, but when he got it, the notes were stuck together."

Morales gazed at the old man a moment, then walked over and sat down beside him on the bench. "Where did the money come from, friend?"

Like most old men, and many people who were not old, this one replied at length. "I helped drag the dead horse from the mud in front of your cantina. I then helped them carry away the dead man, who was head of the

CHAPTER TWENTY-ONE

A Prisoner of the Heart

MARTA WAS RIGHT—and wrong. The town did recover as she had prophesied, but it was a very long process. With the passage of time, individual accounts of experiences added to a general mosaic, but for a long time many who had survived horror and terror preferred not to talk about it, particularly the women of Peralta.

The day after the lawman's return, he and Cap Franklin visited Henry Poole, listened to stories of individual activity, some of it heroic, some of it foolish and reckless, and complied with Henry's request: they sent for the cowman's riding crew, particularly the 'breed Sam Miner. Henry wanted the countryside scouted in all directions; after what he and the others had gone through, he wanted to know for a fact that there were no other marauders in the vicinity.

After leaving Henry, Cap was skeptical. "News travels fast," he told the town marshal. "If there was other bands in the area, they sure as hell aren't here now."

Lee agreed but sent for Poole's riders anyway, after which he went down to his jailhouse just in time to nearly collide with the caféman and his helper, who were emerging from the jailhouse after feeding the prisoners. The caféman put a bleak look on Lee as they passed without speaking.

Lee felt fresh again, a little achy in places but at least rested and fed, bathed and in clean clothing.

He took his time in the jailhouse office. He fired up the little iron stove and made a fresh pot of coffee.

Cap Franklin came to the jailhouse to report that he and Mike Kelly had heard strong talk of lynching the prisoners. The plan was to lure Lee out of town with a story of one of the unaccounted-for renegades hiding in some rocks northeast of town. As soon as the marshal rode away the townsmen would storm the jailhouse, remove the prisoners, take them to the nearest convenient place, and hang them.

Lee went to a window and stood looking out. He turned and sat down at his desk, gazing at the solemn man across from him. "You don't favor hanging?" he asked, and Cap answered, "Oh, I favor hanging. I just don't favor lynching."

Lee was not particularly worried; to his knowledge, no one had ever been taken out of the Peralta *juzgado*, a structure with walls of bake-hardened adobe three feet thick, whose two doors, one in back, the other in front, were doubled oak with huge steel hasps secured by heavy locks. He had no doubt he would be able to safely guard his prisoners until a circuit-riding judge came to town.

He told Cap to keep an eye on things in case it began to really appear a genuine assault was to be made, and assured them he would also be watchful.

Around noon, Marta appeared in his doorway. She'd taken time to soak, fix her hair, and look as she had before the assault on Peralta.

He gestured her toward a chair.

She said, "You look much better."

"I guess the whole town is starting to look and feel a little better."

She smiled. "Yes. Juan was told by an old man who witnessed everything that he knew where the renegades had their sacks of loot. He took Juan to the attic of the storekeeper's house. . . . Juan now has them at his saloon, which he and a hired man have cleaned up."

"I see. Juan sent you to tell me this?"

"Yes. But I also wanted to tell you Lupe Villaverde has the money taken off the dead renegades. Money and rings, personal odds and ends."

Lee faintly frowned. "How did she find those things?"

"I gave them to her. An old woman had them; she gave them to me and I gave them to Lupe."

Lee did not pursue this, although he was baffled by it; if Marta had the effects of the dead renegades, why hadn't she simply brought them with her?

Marta rose. "Lupe will be home this afternoon, if you want to get those things." She began to leave. "Now, Marshal, I've done all I can. The rest is up to you."

Lee shook his head as Marta departed.

When Cap Franklin dropped in again, Lee asked him to guard the prisoners for a little while. Lee headed southward toward the nearest passageway between two buildings in the direction of Mex-town.

The day was not as hot as days had been, thanks to a ground-hugging light breeze from the north. Somewhere a man with a hammer was repairing damage. Elsewhere, making less noise, two other men were gathering broken glass in a small pushcart. Peralta's recovery was progressing.

In Mex-town, Lee reached the *jacal* of Lupe Villaverde, and she opened the door. She did not invite him inside. There were always eyes watching. But she did ask him to step out in the *ramada* shade.

She motioned him toward an old wooden bench and sat nearby in a chair. He asked about the effects from the renegades. She smoothed her skirt and recounted what she had seen and experienced.

While she talked he looked at her, marveling at her beauty and courage.

Lupe looked away when she noticed he was staring. Color rose in her cheeks.

Lee pulled his hat off and turned it with both hands between his knees. Lupe abruptly arose, disappeared inside, and returned with a clean cotton sack. As she placed it between them, she told him it held the possessions that had been taken from the dead *guerilleros* before they were buried.

He nodded. "There is something I don't understand, Lupe. Why didn't Marta give this to me herself?"

Color soared to her cheeks again. She was too flustered to speak. He did not know. Men! Strong as an adobe wall and twice as thick!

She asked if he would like a glass of wine, to which he almost replied that he did not like wine, but when his eyes came up and met her eyes, he said he would like that very much. After she had gone back inside, he leaned his shoulders against the mud wall at his back, put his hat aside, and blew out a long, soundless breath.

When she returned and handed him a glass of red wine, she told him it was from the last gallon her grandfather had made, so they drank to the old man.

Lee finished the wine, declined more, and dumped the hat on his head as he leaned to rise. He said, "I'll take the sack to the jailhouse. Keep it until the town council decides what to do with it."

Lupe nodded, then rose facing him as she said, "I'm very glad you were not hurt."

He remembered Marta commenting that someone had been worried about him. It was as if everything finally fell into place. He leaned, took one of her hands as he told her that she and the others at the cantina had been in more danger than he had been in, and that he was grateful for the miracle that had spared them.

He had touched upon something she had been pondering, and she asked him if he believed in miracles. His answer was neither a common nor a popular one. "They happen, somewhere, every day. Folks call them coincidences."

She squeezed his fingers, and Lee Custis squeezed back.

If you have enjoyed this book and would like to receive details on other Walker Western titles, please write to:

Western Editor
Walker and Company
720 Fifth Avenue
New York, NY 10019